ACCLAIM FOR ANDREW KLAVAN

"Fast paced action and creative world building make this an engaging read beyond the teen market."

—*World Magazine* on *Hostage Run*

"While *MindWar* was very good, *Hostage Run* is even better. Character development, nail-biting suspense, and action keep readers on the edge of their seats, and the ending? You will have to read and see!"

—Redeemed Reader.com

"Edgar Award–winning Klavan's well-orchestrated fantasy thriller features . . . an imaginative mix of gaming action with real-life stakes. With just the right cliff-hanger ending, this trilogy opener shows promise."

—*Booklist* on *MindWar*

". . . the focus is on action, and there's just enough left unresolved to tempt readers onward."

—*Kirkus Reviews* on *MindWar*

"A fantastic read. Fast-paced and wildly imaginative, *MindWar* is a cinematic cyber thriller with more twists than a circuit board."

—John Dixon, author of *Phoenix Island*
(inspiration for the CBS TV show *Intelligence*)

"Klavan retains his James Patterson–like gift for keeping pages turning, and the mystery behind it all . . . is a juicy one, and well handled."

—*Booklist* on *Nightmare City*

"This book will appeal to anyone who is looking for a fast-paced adventure story in which teens must do some fast thinking to survive."

—*School Library Journal* on *If We Survive*

"Klavan turns up the heat for YA fiction . . ."

"The original plot is full of twists and turns and unexpected treasures. Klavan's writing is quick, tight, exciting, and intense. The adrenaline-charged action will keep you totally immersed."

"A thriller that reads like a teenage version of 24 . . . an adrenaline-pumping adventure."

"Action sequences that never let up . . . wrung for every possible drop of nervous sweat."

"[Klavan] is a solid storyteller with a keen eye for detail and vivid descriptive power . . . The Long Way Home is something like 'The Hardy Boys' crossed with the 'My Teacher Is an Alien' series."

"I'm buying everything Klavan is selling, from the excellent first person narrative, to the gut-punching action; to the perfect doses of humor and wit . . . it's all working for me."

"Through it all, Charlie teaches lessons in Christian decency and patriotism, not by talking about those things, or even thinking about them much, but through practicing them . . . Well done, Andrew Klavan."

GAME OVER

GAME OVER

THE MINDWAR TRILOGY

BOOK THREE

ANDREW KLAVAN

THOMAS NELSON
Since 1798

Published in Nashville, Tennessee, by Thomas Nelson. Thomas Nelson is a registered trademark of HarperCollins Christian Publishing, Inc.

Thomas Nelson titles may be purchased in bulk for educational, business, fund-raising, or sales promotional use. For information, please e-mail SpecialMarkets@ThomasNelson.com.

Scripture quotations are taken from The KING JAMES VERSION and The Holy Bible, English Standard Version® (ESV®), copyright © 2001 by Crossway, a publishing ministry of Good News Publishers. Used by permission. All rights reserved.

Publisher's Note: This novel is a work of fiction. Names, characters, places, and incidents are either products of the author's imagination or used fictitiously. All characters are fictional, and any similarity to people living or dead is purely coincidental.

ISBN: 978-1-4016-8900-1 (trade paper)

Library of Congress Cataloging-in-Publication Data

Names: Klavan, Andrew, author.
Title: Game over / Andrew Klavan.
Description: Nashville, Tennessee : Thomas Nelson, [2015] | Series: The MindWar trilogy ; book 3 | Summary: "Rick emerged victorious from The Realm twice. Is his luck about to run out?"-- Provided by publisher.
Identifiers: LCCN 2015028782 | ISBN 9781401688981 (hardback)
Subjects: | CYAC: Virtual reality--Fiction. | Video games--Fiction. | Terrorism--Fiction. | Paralysis--Fiction. | People with disabilities--Fiction. | Christian life--Fiction. | GSAFD: Suspense fiction.
Classification: LCC PZ7.K67823 Gam 2015 | DDC [Fic]--dc23 LC record available at http://lccn.loc.gov/2015028782

Printed in the United States of America

16 17 18 19 20 RRD 5 4 3 2 1

LEVEL ONE:
BAD DREAMS

1. EVIL DEAD

THE CITY WAS empty except for the dead, but the dead were everywhere. Rick saw them staring at him through darkened windows, their jaws slack, their eyes open but lifeless. He saw their bodies lying in the gutters. He saw them sitting slumped at the tables in the outdoor taverns, or lying crumpled in the shop doorways, as if death had found them going out or coming in. He saw the soldiers propped against the courtyard walls, their swords still gripped in their hands, their mouths twisted in an eerie rictus—that fixed grin of slow decay.

Where am I? he thought. His heart was pounding. His head was spinning. *Am I back in the Realm? What part? I've never seen this place before. How did I get here?*

His stare moved over the lifeless forms all around him. These weren't human bodies, not entirely human, anyway. Some were the corpses of those weird half-Boar creatures he had done battle with before, gigantic, tusked pigs that stood on two legs and wielded their weapons with strangely shortened arms that were covered in bristling thick, spiky

3

hair. Others were the dead Cobra Guards; he'd battled them, too, on Kurodar's WarCraft: enormous snakes that could drop from their stunted legs onto their bellies and slither after you with lightning speed and dagger-sharp fangs. And there were some forms, some corpses, he did not recognize. Horrible, human-size bats with the hideous gray faces of ancient crones, wild, wiry hair, and claws like razor blades. They looked like the Harpies he'd seen in books about Greek mythology.

Rick felt confusion rising up inside him, filling him like a kind of fog.

What is this place? How did I get here?

And still he stood staring, staring at the dead. Some of the cadavers had practically rotted to skeletons. Some were worse than that, more horrible, part skeleton, still part flesh. And some were nearly whole. They seemed to have stopped breathing only a moment ago. But wherever he looked, the dead were looking back at him, grinning back at him. It made Rick's stomach sour with disgust.

He began to move down the street. A city street. What city? Where? Was it a dream? He wasn't sure. It didn't feel like a dream. It felt all too real.

He stopped at an intersection of two broad highways. He slowly turned his head, passing his eyes over the scene, squinting in the bright morning light.

Quiet. The whole city was so quiet. Flies buzzing somewhere—he didn't want to know where or around what. And now and then there came a faint breath of wind that carried the foul stench of rotting meat with it. There was no sun visible in the weirdly yellow sky, and yet the sky seemed to radiate heat. It occurred to Rick that even the fresh bodies would not stay fresh for long.

He wanted to get out of here. Fast. Now. But which way? Where to? The fog of confusion filled his mind.

Now he lifted his gaze to the buildings all around him. This was—it had once been—a great city. Golden spires, skyscrapers, domes, and arches soaring into the air. As his eyes traveled over the rising walls of the buildings, his ears slowly became attuned to a different kind of sound, soft within the silence, a steady spatter suggestive of life.

A fountain.

Even in his confusion, his heart rose, his hopes rose. He thought, *She travels by water.*

With that, he lowered his eyes from the building tops—and he saw the corpse standing right in front of him.

His breath caught. It was so close, only a few feet away. One of the Boar Soldiers. And dead—dead most definitely. The pig face and part of the barrel-shaped chest and belly had started to decay. Some of its bones were visible through the ragged flesh. It wasn't breathing. Its eyes were glassy. It was staring and smiling that eerie rigid smile like the others. Definitely dead.

And it was holding a sword.

Stunned, so confused, Rick could only stand there, staring at the thing. It stared back at him.

Then, before he could recover from his shock, it lifted

the sword and swung the blade in a vicious arc toward his throat.

It was a killing blow, meant to sweep his head clean off. The dead Boar Soldier sent up a ghostly echoing squeal as it swung, and Rick screamed, too, in surprise and fear. At the same time, he reacted, moving on pure instinct. Despite the injuries that had ended his football career, he still had the reflexes of a star athlete. He squatted—fast— and the deadly blade swept over him, so close he could feel the breeze of its passing stir his hair.

The instant the sword was past, Rick sprang up straight and—still acting on instinct—stepped in to block the Boar's return stroke. He shoved the beast, both hands hitting its shoulder hard. Being dead, the Boar Soldier did not have much strength or substance—none at all really. The moment Rick touched it, the beast staggered back and fell to the pavement.

Rick turned to run and the second corpse grabbed him, its dead fingers wrapping around his wrist as its grinning, skeletal face leaned in close to him, its mouth wide as if to rip Rick's throat out with its teeth.

Rick let out another cry, a high-pitched cry of animal terror. He tore his wrist free of the dead thing's grip, feeling the claws scrape painfully over his skin.

Then he was running, running fast, his breath coming in panting sobs of panic.

Where was he? What was happening? Was this MindWar? Was it a dream?

Confused, terrified, he could form only one clear thought in his mind, the last thought he'd had before the creatures attacked him:

She travels by water.

He kept thinking the same thing over and over again. He had to find that fountain.

But now all the city's dead were waking. Rising from the seats in the taverns. Grabbing hold of the doorframes for support and slithering to their feet. The Boar Soldiers were picking up their swords. The Cobra Guards—now mostly skeletal snake remains like something you might see in a natural history museum—were slithering toward him over the ground, sluggishly at first, then with increasing speed. Those flying bat-things with the faces of women— the dead, rotten faces of screaming women—lifted into the air and began circling toward him. In whatever direction Rick looked, they were there, coming to life, coming to get him.

He ran to the corner. Dared to stop there for a second. He couldn't hear the fountain over the sound of his own desperate breathing, but the noise had not been far off. It had to be somewhere around here.

He turned to the left—and sure enough he saw it. In an open plaza at the end of the next street, there was a large round basin of rose marble full of silver water. A circle of small geysers flared up out of the water, dancing around a central geyser that shot high into the air. On the far side of the fountain there stood a fanciful building, something out of a fairy tale: half a dozen red spires capped with onion-shaped domes of various designs, some striped red and white, others with diamond ridges of yellow and green, others pure gold.

The plaza was swarming with dead things, walking, slithering, flying. They all seemed to spot Rick at the same moment. And they all came after him.

Rick thought to turn and run, but the dead were behind him, too, slithering over the ground and running toward him and flying at him through the air with hoarse, echoic shrieks of rage. In another moment they would be all over him—their swords, their bared fangs, their sweeping claws. They would tear him to pieces.

He had only one hope. Mariel. And she traveled by water.

He charged toward the fountain. He was sick with fear. He could feel it coursing all through him like a sort of liquid electricity: lightning flashes in the fog of his confusion. But as fearful as he was, he knew he was somehow beyond fear too. Something had happened to him in these months since he had first entered the MindWar Realm. Something had returned to him, in slow stages at first, and then all at once. He wasn't sure what it was exactly, but it felt like a sort of pulsing power at the core of him, a pulsing light that radiated out from his center. Whenever the fear threatened to overwhelm him with its darkness, that power, that light, beat it back and he pushed on.

It was not a new thing. He had always had that power

and light inside him when he had stepped onto the football field in the old days. He lost them for a while after the truck had crashed into his car and shattered his legs. He had retreated to his room, locked the door, drawn the curtains, and played video games hour after hour. But the power and light had returned to him almost fully now; he could feel it. His mother, he knew, would have called it *faith*. Well, *faith* was as good a word as any. Whatever it was, it pushed the fear back, beat by beat, and kept it from taking him over. It gave him strength even as the dead surrounded him.

Using that strength, conquering his fear with it, he ran right into the thick of the attack.

In a few steps the dead were all around him. The ground was alive with them. The sky was dark with them. They besieged him on every side.

Rick plunged through them like a quarterback with the ball, hitting one hard with his shoulder, straight-arming another in the face. Whenever he touched them, they collapsed to the ground. Wherever they fell, a passage of daylight opened before him.

Dodging the flashing swords, the lunging Cobras, the swiping claws of the flying Harpies, he faked left, and charged right, and ran down the corridor of daylight as fast as he could.

He neared the fountain. And, yes, she rose up before him! A thrilling sight. She always was. Beautiful and majestic, queenly and yet warmly kind, Mariel's figure took shape in the silver water and sprang up from the heart of the geyser itself. Instantly, she stretched out her hand to him, and the hand burbled out like mercury until a gleaming sword grew from her fingertips. It was the same sword she had given him before, its graceful hilt ending in a model of her own lovely face.

Rick shouldered another Boar Soldier aside. He cried out and kicked back the head of a Cobra. He straight-armed a Harpy as she screamed down at him. He reached out and grabbed the sword.

The moment his fingers closed around the hilt, he felt a new surge of strength and courage blossoming inside him. It was as if Mariel, in handing him the weapon, had somehow added her unshakable faith to his own.

"Rick! Over here!"

A new voice. He looked up—and there was the sparkling blue form of Favian, his other MindWar friend. The flashing blue sprite was standing in the doorway of the fanciful building. The door was open behind him, and as so often in the past, Favian was beckoning him with a glittery hand: "This way! Come on!"

A Harpy shrieked down at Rick out of the sky, its face half rotten. Rick swung Mariel's blade with all his might, and the face was gone—the head was gone—and the body of the beast came crashing down. A huge skeletal Cobra rose up off the earth, baring its fangs, ready to strike. Rick didn't even pause from the last blow but continued the motion, sweeping the blade back at the Cobra. The sword struck hard, scattering the Cobra's bones in a dozen different directions.

And still the dead came on. Rick had to jump up onto the edge of the fountain's basin to get away from their reaching claws and fangs. Balancing on the slippery marble, he ran around the basin's arc, then leapt off it and onto the building's steps. Another moment and he raced up to where Favian was standing—Favian with his features twisted in anxiety as he stared fearfully at the charging dead. Favian was more of a worrier than a warrior. He had never had much courage. He said so himself. And yet he had somehow always been able to come through when Rick needed him most. He stood his ground now until Rick was beside him.

Then Favian moved like a flash. He always moved like that: like a flash of sparkling blue light, barely substantial. He flashed away through the building's half-open door. And Rick, as he so often did, as he so often had to do to keep from getting himself killed, followed after him.

He was inside. The blue streak of Favian shut the building's door behind him. The cries of the dead outside instantly grew dim. The bright-yellow light of the sky was extinguished. For a few seconds, before his eyes adjusted, Rick couldn't see. The shadows of the interior obscured everything.

Then his vision cleared.

He was in a church, a strange and beautiful church with colorful mosaics covering every inch of the walls. A dark, sad-eyed Virgin Mary gazed at him from a framed painting on one side of him. A sternly frowning Christ peered down at him from the ceiling above.

The main portion of the church—the nave—was open. There were no pews, no statues, only a large floor, which, like the walls, was covered with richly complex and colorful mosaic tiles.

There was nothing else there. Except the sarcophagus. *More dead*, thought Rick.

Indeed, the sarcophagus could have held half a dozen corpses. It was a huge coffin, its sides covered with elaborate mosaics like the ceiling, walls, and floor. It was surrounded by four stout and towering columns, also covered with mosaics. And it was open—the coffin had no lid.

Rick glanced at Favian—Favian, whose face was always pinched with worry and fear. "What is this place?" he asked him. "This city? How did we get here? I can't remember . . ."

Favian's figure of fluctuating blue light shimmered. "Mariel and I had to sneak in when the darkness spread."

"The darkness?"

"It spread over everything everywhere," Favian told him. "The Scarlet Plain. The Blue Wood. The Ruins. Everything. This is all that's left: the Golden City. It's all that's left of MindWar."

"The Golden City," Rick murmured. The heart of MindWar, the battery that fed the place with energy. But why was it full of dead creatures? And what was this darkness Favian was talking about?

He did not really understand, but he turned away from Favian, back to the sarcophagus. He had the powerful sense that he should look inside, that he had to look inside—and at the same time, he knew that he very much did not want to look inside, not ever. He felt as if he were in one of those dreams where you have to do what you know you shouldn't do.

He took a long breath. He could still hear dead things outside the church. They were pounding on the great wooden door, crying for his blood. He ignored them. He stepped deeper into the building, deeper into the shadow, closer to the sarcophagus.

Favian flashed along by his side.

"I don't think you should do that," he said. "Really. Don't look in there."

Rick ignored him. He kept moving toward the enormous coffin.

"This place, this church. It's so strange," said Favian, worried. "Like a ghost church or something . . ."

Rick still didn't answer. All his attention was focused on the sarcophagus. It was drawing him, pulling him to it.

He reached it now. Holding his sword in one hand, he put his other hand on the edge and leaned over the side to take a look.

He gasped at what he saw. He could barely comprehend.

The sarcophagus was full . . . of nothingness. An impenetrable, incomprehensible darkness. A darkness that went down and down forever, deeper than death itself.

13

Rick stood staring into it as if hypnotized. He felt something inside him drop open like a trapdoor, all his courage falling through it into that eternal nothingness.

And suddenly, like a great wave, the dark swarmed up out of the coffin and seized him.

2. THE AWAKENED

RICK'S EYES FLASHED open and he started screaming. He reached out frantically in a panic. Was he being swallowed by the darkness? Had the nothingness claimed him forever? Was he dead? Was he in hell?

He fought off the panic. He touched his chest with his hands. He felt his heart pounding, his lungs heaving as he gasped for breath.

Alive! he thought. *I'm still alive!*

He lifted himself up on one elbow and looked around him. He saw his desk, his laptop. His jeans and sweatshirt crumpled on the floor. He saw his football posters and football calendar tacked onto the wall. The harsh glare of sunlight was breaking through the parting of the curtains over his window.

He was in his bedroom. In his family's house. In the MindWar compound. Safe. Alive.

His heart slowing, he sat up on the edge of his bed.

Another dream, he thought.

The dreams came every night now, every night since his return from MindWar. Each one of them was more realistic than the last. Each time he woke it was more impossible to believe it had not been real, that he had not been somehow swept into the MindWar Realm again without using the portal. Which was impossible. So yeah, it had to be a dream. But it sure did seem like the real deal.

Now the headache hit. Of course. Like the dreams, they were coming every day, more powerful each time. This one felt like someone had stuck his thumbs into his eyes and ripped his skull open. Rick sucked in a breath through his clenched teeth. He pressed his temples with his thumbs. Closed his eyes. Massaged his brow with his fingers.

He knew the headache would pass. He knew the dream would fade too. But they would both come back, stronger and more real than ever.

Because of the Realm. Because he had spent too much time in the MindWar Realm, a computerized world created by a terrorist named Kurodar, built out of a link between Kurodar's mind and a bank of supercomputers, a way for the killer to imagine himself into any computer system on the planet and take it over. Unless Rick could stop him.

The Realm had infected Rick's brain somehow, causing these dreams, these headaches. And the infection was getting worse.

That thought made something curdle in the pit of Rick's stomach. If there was one thing in this world he didn't want, it was Kurodar's sick imagination poisoning his own. Not much was known about the terrorist, but they knew this: he was a highly not-nice person. He had already tried to crash several jets into a city, kidnap Rick's father, and blow up Washington, DC. And for Rick, the idea of having the imagination of a guy like that digging like a worm inside his own brain was sickening.

He didn't want to tell anyone what was happening to him. He was afraid Commander Mars, or his lieutenant, Miss Ferris, would take him out of the fight, forbid him to return to the Realm. Rick's father—the physicist code-named "Traveler"—had guessed the truth and was looking for a cure. In the meantime, Rick could only hope the symptoms would pass and he would recover over time.

For the moment, anyway, the throbbing pain inside his head was beginning to recede a little. Rick thought he might be able to get up, wash up, get dressed, go outside, and join Mom and Raider for breakfast.

He began to lower his hands from his head . . . And as he did, his mouth opened and he stopped breathing as a new sickness of fear filled him.

"What?" he whispered. "What???"

His wrist! His right wrist! There were marks on it. Four lines of red, with purple bruising already staining the skin around them.

The second he saw them, Rick knew what those marks were. He remembered the dead Boar Soldier in his dream, the one who had grabbed him, the one who had torn his flesh as he broke free of its grip . . .

Those were its marks. Its claw marks on Rick's wrist.

Rick touched the marks with his fingertips. He felt the ridges of his scraped flesh. He felt the pain. It was impossible but true: The marks were there. They were real.

And this was no dream!

3.   ARCANE HEARTS

RICK ALWAYS TRIED to show a cheerful face to his brother. Nine-year-old Raider was so relentlessly upbeat and energetic himself that Rick simply didn't have the heart to bring him down. The kid had a beaming, freckled, pie plate of a face, with dark hair spilling sloppily down over his forehead, and a mouth that never seemed to stop moving—especially now, as he ate and yammered at the same time.

"So if I get the new box for Christmas, I'm thinking we should be able to spend about a week just totally destroying the latest Luigi Haunted House, which is supposed to be completely epic, and I read in *Game Master* that they may even reboot the old Mario Newsman series, which would be awesome times ten, and then we could . . ."

This went on and on as Raider sat at the breakfast table and shoveled cereal into his maw, somehow managing to talk, chew, and swallow all at once without ever interrupting one to do the other.

Rick sat across from him, moving his fork listlessly through the scrambled eggs on his plate. He was trying to stop thinking about those scratch marks on his arm. Those scratch marks hidden underneath his sweatshirt sleeve. Those impossible scratch marks. From a living dead Boar Soldier. Who couldn't exist outside the Realm. Who had only been in a dream. Who had left marks on his arm . . .

He wasn't doing a very good job of not thinking about it.

His mom was standing at the sink, the morning light from the window turning her straw-colored hair into a kind of Mom Halo. She was rinsing the dishes off to put in the dishwasher and had her back to the table. But now and then she would glance over her shoulder at Rick and smile a little at the way he patiently absorbed Raider's constant chatter. This time, though, when she looked back, she saw Rick toying with his food and silently lifted her chin at his plate: *Eat something.*

Rick took a forkful of eggs and stuck it in his mouth, swallowing without tasting it, for her sake. But the sight of those marks on his arm . . . It had killed his appetite. The Boar Soldier was dead. He was in a dream! How could he leave scratches on his wrist? How could it happen? What could it mean?

He had to talk to his dad. His dad was the only person who might have some clue what was happening.

He quickly swallowed a few more forkfuls of eggs, then pushed back his chair and got up from the table. Raider was still talking. Rick thumped him on top of the head with his fist, thump, thump, thump.

"Yo. Earth to Raider. I gotta go save the world. Hold that thought."

The idea that Raider could hold that, or any, thought without releasing it through his mouth was ridiculous. But Rick knew he could come back hours from now and pick up the same sentence at a later stage and get the general idea of what the kid was thinking about.

Which would be Christmas, of course. Because while in MindWar, everything was bizarreness and danger 24/7, here in RL—Real Life—Christmas was only a week and a half away. The thought of the presents and the food, not to mention the food and the presents, pretty much dominated every second of Raider's waking consciousness.

Mom had done everything she could to keep RL as normal as possible. As soon as they'd moved into their little green-and-white barracks house in the MindWar compound, she hurried to decorate it with family photos and homey furniture to make it look like their old house back in Putnam Hills. Now, too, she had somehow managed to put out their usual Christmas decorations: the white fairy lights around the windows, the frosted angels on the glass, the manger scene on the lampstand in the living room, and, of course, the tree, which Rick, Raider, and Dad had cut down in the surrounding forest and which now stood in the living room corner. After Rick had managed— just barely—to escape the Realm last time, they had all celebrated by breaking out their boxes of old ornaments and hanging them from the branches. Even Rick himself had to admit the decorated tree achieved a high level of Christmas awesomeness.

But the moment Rick stepped out of the house, this homey atmosphere vanished. The MindWar compound was a secret military installation hidden in a vast, dense forest owned by the federal government. On the surface, it was a collection of barracks surrounded by barbed wire, with guard towers here and there, armed guards inside the glassed cubicles on top. It looked pretty much like any Army camp and about as un-Christmassy as you could get. But that was only on the surface. Most of the place was underground and even less Christmassy, if that was possible: just a vast network of buried windowless corridors and rooms housing the people and technology required to send MindWarriors into Kurodar's universe.

Or MindWarrior, singular. Rick was now the only one. But there had been three others before him, as he'd now discovered . . . and that was the other thing on his mind, the other thing he needed to talk to his dad about.

So he headed for the infirmary.

It was cold outside now, really cold. The sky was uniformly gray and there were flurries of snow in the air. The surrounding forest was pale green, the leafless trees sapping the color from the interspersed firs and hemlocks and pines. The usual security teams stationed outside some of the more important buildings had gone indoors. Only the tower guards and the guards around the perimeter remained visible.

The infirmary was a large barracks against the fence on one side of the compound. It looked the same as most of the other barracks except it was painted light red instead of green and white and there was a red cross over the entrance. The guards now stationed just within the door did not even flinch as Rick walked by them. Everyone knew him here. In a way, he was the reason why the entire camp existed.

With a nod to the receptionist at the front desk, he continued down the narrow hallway to the Recovery Wing. His father was already there, in the waiting area outside the last room in the barracks. Rick had expected that. But he had not expected to see Professor Jameson with him.

Jameson, his dad's old friend, had been the head of the Physics Department at Putnam Hills University where his dad had worked. The two scientists had been working on CBI—computer-brain interface—the possibilities of linking the human imagination with computers. It was during that work that Rick's dad stumbled on Kurodar's Realm. Having alerted his old college girlfriend Leila Kent, now an intelligence officer in the State Department, the Traveler had gone underground to invent the technology needed to invade the Realm and wage MindWar.

So that's who Professor Jameson was. But more importantly, he was also Molly's father. And if he was here, then Molly was probably here as well.

Jameson and Rick's dad saw Rick coming and quickly stopped talking. They turned to greet him with bright smiles. The Traveler was the smaller of the two, a short, narrow man, bald, with thick glasses—very unlike his broad, tall, athletic son. Jameson was bigger and more disheveled. He could never keep his last few strands of hair properly combed or keep his shirt from coming untucked around his paunch. A big, slouched, sloppy St. Bernard of a man.

Professor Jameson reached out and shook Rick's hand in both of his, meeting his eyes with a meaningful look. Rick had saved his daughter's life barely a week ago—shattered the very boundaries of the Realm to sweep her out of a closing ring of enemy gunmen. Rick wasn't sure how much the professor had been told about the adventure, but it seemed he'd been told something, judging by the look of affection and gratitude in his eyes.

Rick shook hands with him and turned to his father. "How's Victor One doing?" he asked.

"Better," said the Traveler. "They're in there."

They? thought Rick, and an unpleasant feeling fanned out over his chest. He didn't want to admit to himself what the feeling was, but it was hard to avoid the truth: it was jealousy. He turned and looked through the doorway and . . . yup, it was jealousy all right. Now he was sure.

Victor One, the Traveler's personal bodyguard, had heroically gone in search of Molly when she'd been kidnapped by Kurodar's operatives. The two of them had fought side by side in a desperate battle to survive. Victor One was a cool, tough, ex-military man. Not to mention craggily handsome. Also not to mention relaxed and witty in a way the intense, passionately competitive Rick could never hope to be. Rick had brought both Molly and Victor One to safety in the end, but not before the bodyguard had taken a bullet in the chest, about two inches from his heart. A bad injury. If Victor One had come any closer to dying, he'd have to buy a harp. But now, only a week later, he was starting to mend. He lay on the narrow hospital bed, pale but awake and alert. He had a half smile on his rugged face. And his humorous blue eyes were trained on Molly.

Molly was sitting at the foot of the bed, smiling down at him, talking softly. She looked good—to Rick, she always looked good. She was tall, nearly six feet, and had a powerful athlete's build. But her face was delicate and pretty, with soft brown eyes and a small nose peppered with faint freckles. She was wearing a purple-pink sweater and white jeans, which struck Rick as appealingly girly—and made him more jealous still. In fact, the sight of her—the sight of her there with Victor One—hit Rick hard in all kinds of ways he didn't want to think about.

There had been a moment before all this crazy MindWar stuff happened . . . a moment when Rick, to his own surprise, had found himself kissing Molly, their long friendship suddenly melding into something else, something more. But whatever their relationship was and whatever it was about to become, it all pretty much ended when his legs were shattered. After that, after he lost his football life, he didn't want to see Molly at all. Or, that is, he didn't think Molly would be interested in him. And he didn't want her pity, that was for sure.

And then, in the Realm, he met Mariel.

There was nothing like Mariel in RL. The majestic, beautiful silver spirit who gave him strength and weapons when he needed them, who taught him how to use his spirit to manipulate and transform the Realm's substance . . . Rick's feelings for Mariel were incredibly powerful—but what were those feelings exactly? Every time he saw her, his heart filled up—but with what? Was it love? Could you even love a computer-world water spirit? Could he ever bring her back with him into RL?

So he'd met Mariel . . . and then he saw Molly again . . . and some of his old feelings for her had started coming back . . . and now, he saw her with Victor One, smiling down at Victor One, him smiling back up at her . . .

Confusing, confusing, confusing . . . especially after what he'd discovered in the hidden room in the underground corridors of the compound . . . the two glass coffins down there . . . the weirdest thing . . .

Rick put something like an easygoing expression on his face and strolled into the hospital room looking as if Victor One and Molly could get married on the spot without causing him a care in the world.

"Hey," said Victor One, his voice hoarse. He lifted a hand weakly in greeting. "There's the hero of the hour."

Molly stood up from the bed quickly, as if Rick had caught her doing something wrong. Her cheeks flushed red.

Rick thought, *Hey, no worries. If you're into Victor One, you're into him, no big deal, no reason to get all blushy about it.*

That's what he thought, not what he felt. What he felt was . . . confusing . . .

"Hey, Mol," he said casually—and then he quickly looked away from her to give her a chance to recover her composure. "How you feeling, V-One?"

"Like some clown shot me in the chest. How 'bout you? How're you feeling?"

"Like some gigantic flying octopus chased me through space while enemy fighters tried to ray-gun me to death. Otherwise, great."

"We can compare scars," said Victor One with something between a cough and a laugh.

Molly now spoke up. "Victor has been using his downtime to do some really interesting research."

She sounded proud of him. Rick didn't like the sound. "Oh yeah?" he said as cheerfully as he could. "What've you found out?"

"Well, lying around bleeding all day gave me a lot of time to think," V-One said softly. "I've been worried that there may be a traitor in the MindWar Project."

Rick nodded. They were all worried about that.

Victor One continued, "So it occurred to me to wonder: that house in the woods where the kidnappers imprisoned Molly . . . that barn where Kurodar hid the Breach into the Realm . . . all those acres of swamp and forest where everything was so well hidden . . . Who owned that land?"

Rick tilted his head. He had to admit it was a good question. Victor One wasn't just tough and brave (and ruggedly handsome), he was also smart.

So what? he thought. *If she's into him, she's into him . . . I'll always have my computerized dream girl who's probably not even real . . .*

"I linked up with some of my military intelligence pals," the bodyguard continued. "The land ownership was well hidden behind a lot of dummy companies, but we finally traced it to a dude named Theodore Moros. Greek-American businessman in his seventies. Made, like, a gazillion dollars in the aerospace industry. Now gives it away to a lot of supposedly good causes."

"Like Kurodar trying to blow up America?" Rick said.

"Yeah, that didn't strike me as such a good cause either. I'm thinking if my intelligence pal can help me get inside Mr. Moros's computers, I might be able to find out what else he's been spending his money on. I might even make a little unexpected visit to Mr. Moros's mansion on this Caribbean island he owns . . ."

"There is no way you are getting out of that bed until you're completely better," said Molly.

And the way she said it—like a tender, caring girlfriend—made Rick glad that his hair couldn't actually spontaneously burst into flames—because if it could have, it would have, which would have been very difficult to explain.

Well, here was the thing (so Rick told himself): if Molly was in love with V-One now, Rick had no business complaining about it or getting jealous about it or anything like that. He had avoided Molly. Ignored her. And he'd gotten all . . . let's say *fascinated* . . . He'd gotten all fascinated with the beautiful Mariel. And it wasn't Molly's fault if Mariel had turned out to be . . .

What exactly *had* Mariel turned out to be? That was the question that had been bedeviling Rick ever since he found those glass coffins. Mariel had been so much to him, meant so much to him, but now . . . now that he'd seen what was in the coffins . . .

Rick had only recently found out about the three MindWarriors who'd been sent into the Realm before him. One of them had died in Kurodar's weird world. Rick had seen the poor guy's Realm self rotting in the Spider-Snake tunnels beneath the Scarlet Plain. The other two—so Rick now believed—were Favian and Mariel.

When Rick had returned from his last Realm immersion, he had gone in search of the truth. He'd used a flash drive his father had given him to override the MindWar compound's security. He had made his way through the maze-like tunnels of the compound. He had come to a secret room at the compound's center. And that's where he had found the two glass coffins, foggy inside with refrigeration mist.

In one of those coffins, he had discovered the body of a

short, stocky black man. The man was lying in suspended animation, but still breathing. Peering through the mist, Rick recognized him immediately as the RL version of the blue sprite Favian. Which meant that the other coffin . . .

The other coffin held Mariel. His heart had sped up as he moved to the edge of the box. What would her RL self look like? Would she be as beautiful as she was in the Realm? Would she be older? Younger? Would there be a wedding band on her finger?

He came to the edge of the coffin and looked inside. His breath caught. His eyes went wide.

There was nothing there. Nothing except a box. It was a plastic black box. It had blue lights that flashed dimly beneath its shiny surface. It seemed to be some kind of computerized device or something.

Rick wasn't sure what it was, but he had to wonder: was that machine the real Mariel? Was that all she was: a computer-generated image of a human being? Had Rick formed an infatuation with an illusion? Had he given up Molly—the real, warm, human Molly—for someone who wasn't even there?

Rick turned to Molly now. He didn't know what he was going to say to her, but he felt that he had to say something, something to let her know it was okay if she was in love with Victor One, that whatever happened, he just wanted her to be happy. He wanted to make sure she knew that. Even though it wasn't true.

He opened his mouth to speak, but he never found out

what he was going to say. Before a word could cross his lips, there were two sharp raps on the door.

Rick looked over his shoulder and saw his father standing there, Jameson hovering just behind him.

"Mars wants us," the Traveler said. "We've got to go."

4. MARS

THE BEAST WAS huge and hideous. Thrashing tentacles that seemed to reach for miles across the blackness. A single eye glaring from the end of each tentacle. And above them all, a tremendous globular head, its enormous eyes so full of hatred and rage they seemed to burn with a white fire.

It had been little more than a week since Rick had killed the Octo-Guardian, but already he had forgotten just how horrible a creature it was. Seeing it now again in the 3-D holographic theater in the compound's underground auditorium made his throat feel tight with disgust. The thing looked as if it were right there in front of him.

He watched as his own image—a 3-D image of himself closed inside the cockpit of a small fighter plane—charged directly at the Octo-Guardian's head, firing at the beast's raging eyes. He could almost feel the auditorium shake around him as the monster keeled over sideways in space and went crashing down to the Realm's surface far below.

Then, as Rick continued watching, his holographic self turned his aircraft toward the Breach: an opening Kurodar had created between the Realm and RL. Through that opening, Rick could see where Molly and Victor One were huddled together in the woods, a circle of armed men closing in on them, ready to wipe them out. In another moment, Rick knew, his hologram would fly his aircraft straight into the Breach and burst impossibly out of MindWar and into reality in order to pull Molly and V-One from the gunmen's clutches . . .

But before that could happen, the three-dimensional picture froze. It just stopped moving completely. A moment later, the lights of the auditorium came up, and there on the stage stood the director of the MindWar Project, Commander Jonathan Mars. Mars was looking directly at Rick, and his eyes were nearly as full of rage as the Octo-Guardian's had been.

Mars was a forbidding figure at the best of times. He was in his fifties, with a face that looked like it was carved out of rock then decorated with iron. He had craggy features under silver-gray hair, deep-set humorless eyes under bushy silver-gray eyebrows, and a mouth that seemed to have been chiseled into the space above his chin in a permanent frown.

"I'm not going to ask you what you were thinking," he said. "Because I already know." His grumbling voice was quiet, but Rick could hear the fury in it all the same. "You were thinking you would be a hero. You were thinking you would save the day."

"I was thinking my friends were about to be killed . . ."

"You were thinking like a child," Mars said right over him. "Hundreds of thousands of lives are at stake here— millions of lives! The security of your country. The security of weapons systems that could virtually wipe out life on earth if they fell into the wrong hands. And you violated every protocol we have in order to save two people. Your friends!"

Rick was about to answer, but the words died on his lips. It did sound pretty stupid when Mars put it that way. He supposed he ought to say he was sorry he'd done it. But he wasn't sorry. Given the same situation, he'd do it again. So there was not much point in saying sorry, was there?

"Do you have any idea the risk you took?" Mars went on, glaring at him from under those impressive eyebrows.

Rick shrugged. He had flown his Realm craft into the face of a bunch of machine gun–toting thugs, so yes, he was pretty well aware of the risk. "I've been back more than a week. Why are you bringing this up now?"

Mars didn't answer. He shook his head. He said, "You're the only MindWarrior we have left. That makes you the only chance we've got to stop Kurodar before he strikes full force. If we lose you, we lose everything . . ."

"Look, I know—"

"You don't know," Mars said, cutting him off. "You can't know because nobody knows. Nobody knows the long-term effects of being immersed in the Realm. That's bad enough. But the moment you rode that ship through the Breach . . ." Mars fell silent and shook his head.

"What?" said Rick. He felt his stomach tighten at Mars's unfinished sentence. The headaches that were getting so bad . . . the dreams that were getting so real . . . Had flying through the Breach made them worse? Had that somehow amped up the side effects of long-term exposure to the Realm? "The moment I rode my ship through the Breach—what?" he asked again.

Mars kept shaking his head. "I don't know. Like I said. No one knows. Kurodar built the MindWar Realm to allow him to imagine himself into our computer systems. His brain, your brain, the computers, they're all linked together when you're in there. When you went through the Breach, for that one second, you and Kurodar were completely linked together . . ."

"All right," said Rick's dad quietly. "That's enough." The man code-named the Traveler was sitting in the chair next to Rick. He was watching Commander Mars with a mild expression, his calm eyes blinking occasionally behind his glasses, giving no emotion away. Rick knew his dad and Mars did not get along very well. As in not at all. "There's no point in scaring him," his dad went on. "We've spent the last week scanning his brain for any abnormalities. There aren't any."

"That we know of," muttered Mars.

"That's right. So we have no reason to think there'll be any problem at all. Rick risked his life to save two friends. That's the sort of person he is. If he weren't that sort of person, it wouldn't have been worth sending him into the Realm in the first place."

Rick watched as the corners of Mars's lips pulled down in a spasm of barely controlled anger. He was not a man who liked to be challenged, especially not by some nerdy computer geek like the Traveler. Mars thought he knew what was best—for the project, for his staff, even for the country. In some ways, he thought he *was* the country, that to stand up against him was to stand against America itself. Just then, Rick thought if Mars could have shot his dad dead, he might've done it. It wasn't such a far-fetched idea. Mars had already pulled a gun on the Traveler once before.

All the same, Mars dropped the subject now and moved on to the real subject of the meeting. "Anyway, that's not the reason I called you here. We're expecting another attack."

Rick sat up straight, surprised. That explained why Mars's always-simmering anger had suddenly flared like this. "Another attack already?" he said. "I just delivered Kurodar a major fail . . ."

"That's the problem apparently. Our spies in the Axis are telling us that Kurodar is getting desperate. Rick blew up his fortress . . . downed his WarCraft . . . and now the Axis Assembly has decided to pull their funding for the MindWar. They're tired of pouring money into something that doesn't work."

"Well, that's a good thing, right?" Rick said with what he hoped was an annoying shrug.

"It could be," Mars replied through gritted teeth. "But Kurodar says he doesn't need the Assembly anymore. He says he has a secret weapon that will allow him to act on his own."

"What sort of weapon?" said the Traveler, and while his eyes remained calm, he leaned forward slightly in his seat.

"We don't know," said Mars. "Kurodar apparently swore to the Assembly he would prove the effectiveness of the MindWar Realm by pulling off an attack on our country all by himself—an attack so vast, so destructive, he said, that the Assembly would see once and for all that MindWar is the way to bring us to our knees."

Rick wasn't sure why, but when he heard this, Favian's voice seemed to speak into his mind.

The darkness spread over everything everywhere. The Scarlet Plain. The Blue Wood. The Ruins. The Golden City is all that's left of MindWar.

That's what Favian had said in his dream. But so what? What did it have to do with this new attack Mars was talking about? And anyway, it was just a dream. Wasn't it? Rick rubbed the sleeve of his sweatshirt, feeling the scratches on his wrist underneath.

"So you have to send me back in," he said.

Mars glared at him—it reminded Rick of the way the Octo-Guardian glared at him. "If we can trust you," he said.

GAME OVER

A flash of anger went through Rick. He was never very good at controlling his temper, especially around pompous authority figures like Mars. He jumped to his feet, ignoring the dull ache that still went through his legs sometimes, especially when he moved too quickly. "What's that supposed to mean?" he said.

"We're still trying to assess the damage that's been done to your brain . . ."

"There is no damage," Rick said—though he was nowhere near sure of that. "You have to send me back in."

"I don't have to do anything," said Mars. "If your mind was somehow altered by going through the Breach, sending you back could cause more damage than it prevents."

"I need to get back into the Realm," said Rick. His heart felt like a clenched fist in his chest. "I won't leave Favian and Mariel to die in there. I can't. I've got to find a way to get them out."

Mars gave a rough snort. "More friends."

"That's right. And I promised Mariel—"

"Ah, Mariel!" Mars cut him off dismissively. His permanent frown seemed to turn upward in a chiseled sneer. "Don't you understand? There is no Mariel. There never was."

With that, Mars turned on his heel and stormed out of the auditorium.

5. GLASS TOWER

THERE WAS A little grove of trees planted outside the Dials' house, a small cluster of oaks and elms and maples that had been set there to enhance the view from inside. When the Dials were in the house, they could look out, and the trees' branches partially blocked the sight of the barbed wire and the guard towers that surrounded them. It was a nice effect. It made the family feel less like prisoners of the MindWar Project.

Now Rick was standing under the trees with his hands in his pockets and his shoulders hunched against the cold. The temperature was dropping steadily as the sun was dropping toward the western horizon. Rick shivered a little, his breath misting in front of him. Lost in thought, he watched the guard tower through the branches, his eyes on the glassed-in booth at the top. Inside the booth, Rick could see the guard pacing back and forth. He would come to the glass wall nearest Rick and look out over the compound, then he would move off to the other side of the booth, out of Rick's line of sight. A few moments would pass. After presumably scanning the forest outside the

41

barbed wire, the guard would come pacing back into view again.

"Mars is right, isn't he?" the Traveler said. "Your symptoms—your headaches—they've gotten worse since you went through the Breach, haven't they?"

Rick barely nodded in answer.

"And the nightmares—do they still seem real?"

Slowly, Rick turned to him. His father was hunkered inside a blue overcoat. He had a black woolen watch cap pulled down over his bald head. The little puffs of frost that came out of his mouth as he breathed rose up and fogged his glasses.

Without answering him, Rick opened his own overcoat and pulled his arm out of the sleeve. He rolled up his sweatshirt sleeve and held out his bared wrist so his father could see the scratches there.

The Traveler let out a long breath. Gently, he took hold of his son's hand. He frowned as he turned Rick's arm back and forth, examining the marks. "Tell me what you dreamed," he said.

Rick turned to look up at the guard tower booth again. The soldier inside looked out through the glass wall, then turned and paced away out of sight.

"I dreamed about the Golden City," said Rick.

"The Realm's battery," his father murmured, studying his arm. "The place where Kurodar's imagination enters the Realm and powers it."

"Right. In my dream, it was littered with dead security

42

bots. Creatures Kurodar had imagined into being. He had withdrawn his energy from them, and their corpses were rotting. But when Kurodar sensed my presence, he brought them back to life and sent them after me. One of them—a dead Boar warrior—grabbed my arm. When I pulled away, his claws scratched my wrist."

Rick still didn't turn back as his father examined the marks. He kept watching the booth. The soldier paced back into view through the glass.

He could hear the concern in his father's voice. "You dreamed that? And when you woke up . . . ? These marks . . . ?"

Rick nodded, still without turning. "Yeah. When I woke up, the scratches were there."

The soldier in the booth looked out the glass for a moment, then turned and paced away out of sight.

Rick glanced over at his father now. His dad's cheeks expanded as he blew out another long, whistling breath.

"What's happening to me?" Rick asked him. He could hear his own voice trembling. It wasn't just from the cold. It was fear too. He sounded like a little boy afraid of the dark.

His father examined the wounds some more. He didn't answer.

"What did Mars mean about Mariel?" Rick asked. "That there is no Mariel. That's true, isn't it? Otherwise, why was her coffin empty except for that black box? What was that thing? Who is Mariel, Dad?"

He had asked his father these questions before—after

he had seen the empty coffin. But his father had put off answering them. He wasn't sure, he said. He needed to get more information, he said. Rick had waited to hear what his dad had found out. But he couldn't wait anymore. Everything was too confused. He was beginning to be unsure of what was real and what was not. In his life, in his mind, in his heart—everywhere.

His father sighed and let go of Rick's hand. As Rick slipped his arm back inside his overcoat, his dad said, "I'm still not sure. Mars is not exactly quick with a straight answer. He won't tell me much, but I got some of it out of him and I think I can guess the rest." Rick's dad, quiet as he was, absentminded as he was, was also one of the strongest, most self-assured people Rick had ever met. It was his faith, Rick knew. His faith seemed to fill him up, from inside somehow, to keep him strong and tranquil no matter what was happening around him. Now his confidence gave Rick confidence too.

Bundled up inside his overcoat again, Rick shoved his hands into his pockets and lifted his eyes to the guard tower, watching the soldier up there pace as he listened to his father speaking.

"When I first stumbled upon Kurodar's Realm," the Traveler said, "I handed over much of my work to Leila Kent, and she passed it on to Mars. Included in that work were our BCI experiments, our attempts at full brain-computer interface. There were experimental files Professor Jameson and I had created in which we'd tried to download the minds of several hundred volunteers and translate them into a form that could be read by a computer. *Connectomes*, they're called."

"Yeah, I remember. I was one of the volunteers. Most of my friends did it too. You made those things of all of us."

"That's right. Just about everyone we knew helped out by hooking their brains up to our computers, and we made connectomes of them, or tried to. There were also plenty of strangers we just recruited for the experiment."

"Okay," said Rick. "What happened then?"

In the booth above the winter branches of the trees, the soldier paced out of sight again.

"Mars acted too quickly," the Traveler went on—and even without looking at him, Rick could hear the irritation in his voice. "He felt the security situation was urgent and he had to act. Even before I could fully complete programming a system that would safely immerse our MindWarriors into the Realm, Mars jumped the gun and sent three subjects in without my knowledge."

"Subjects . . . You mean people. MindWarriors like me. Mariel, Favian, and the other guy, the one I saw in the Spider-Snake tunnel."

"The man you call Favian was a young man named Fabian Child, an Army clerk who happened to have tremendous gaming skills. Mars thought he might be able to help even though he wasn't really a warrior. He wasn't even very courageous . . ."

"No, I know," said Rick with a little smile, thinking

of Favian's perpetually worried look. "But he's courageous enough, it turns out. More than he thinks, anyway." He kept gazing up at the glass booth at the top of the tower. And the soldier kept pacing back and forth within.

"The other man was a United States Marine sergeant named James Posner. A decorated combat veteran, plenty tough and plenty brave, but not much of a gamer."

"What about Mariel?" said Rick. "Tell me about Mariel." He actually held his breath, waiting for his father's reply.

"Mariel," his father said slowly, "was not a person at all. She was a program. I'm not sure whether Mars used one of our connectomes or whether he combined two or several of them together. He won't tell me. But the mission was so dangerous, Mars wanted to experiment with sending in a connectome rather than a real person. If he could stop Kurodar with programs instead of people, he thought he could reduce the risk of casualties. You can't blame him for that. He was looking to save lives."

"No, you can't blame him," Rick tried to say, but the words wouldn't come out. He could barely speak. He could barely take in the information. His head felt like it was filled with mist. Mariel. A program. A "connectome." Not a real woman. Not an actual person at all. Which meant that all those feelings he had for her . . .

"The mission was a disaster," his father went on. "The MindWarriors were immersed without full security. They'd barely traveled ten yards from the portal when one of Kurodar's security bots spotted them and attacked."

"The Spider-Snake," Rick whispered hoarsely. He—who had twice the gaming skills of Fabian Child combined with at least some of the courage of Marine sergeant James Posner—had only just barely outrun the thing and defeated it . . . and even then, he had needed Mariel's and Favian's help.

"Sergeant Posner was killed trying to defend the others from the Spider-Snake," his father said. "And Mariel and Favian were wounded so badly, their minds were cut off from their portals. Mars lost connection with them and there's been no way to extract them."

Rick nodded dumbly. He had seen Posner in the tunnel . . . or what was left of him. And as for Favian and Mariel . . . "They're getting weaker every day," he said. "They don't even remember who they are . . ." The words brought a new thought into his mind. A new thought with new pain. "Mariel doesn't know," he whispered. He stared up through the branches at the soldier pacing in the guard tower booth. "She doesn't know she's not real, does she? She doesn't know she's just a computer download." The idea was a special agony to him. The image of Mariel rose in his mind: her warmth, her grace, her strength, her beauty. "She thinks she's a human being," he said. "She thinks I'm going to save her and reconnect her to her body and . . ."

Standing beside him, his father shook his head sadly. "I don't know. Probably. That's probably what she thinks."

Rick had to pause a few moments to subdue the waves of sorrow that were washing over him. Ever since Mariel and Favian had been injured, their energy had been slowly bleeding out of them, their Realm selves aging quickly toward a horrible living death. But Mariel had hope. Her hope was Rick. She believed he was a hero who had come to save her. She believed he had been sent to rescue her from her dying Realm life. She didn't realize that her Realm life was the only life she had ever had, the only life she was ever going to have. Bring her out of the Realm, and Mariel would be nothing, some electronic impulses, some numbers flashing in a box. Nothing.

Rick went on gazing up at the guard tower. He didn't want to face his father. He didn't want his father to see the pain and misery in his eyes. He gazed up at the guard tower, and slowly, something occurred to him . . .

The soldier. The pacing soldier. He had come to the glass window again a few moments ago. He had looked out and paced away again out of sight . . . and he had stayed out of sight. He had been gone a long time now. Too long. Rick kept looking up there, waiting for him to pace back into view, and he didn't. Seconds went by and more seconds, and he didn't reappear. Rick murmured, "Where is he?"

He heard his father say, "What?"

"That soldier," Rick said, his voice still low. He was thinking—thinking fast—trying to figure it out. Maybe it was a change of shift or something. Or maybe the guy had paused to get a drink of water or a snack. But something deep down inside him told him it wasn't that. It was something else. Something wrong . . .

"What's the matter?" his father asked him, following his gaze to look up at the tower.

Rick shook his head a little. "Nothing, I . . ."

Before he could finish, he saw a movement in the high booth. A reflection on the glass. The soldier was moving back into position.

There he is! Rick thought with relief.

The soldier came into full view, looking out through the glass of the booth. And all of Rick's relief vanished.

Because it was not the soldier anymore. It was not even a human being!

It was a giant humanoid Boar! It was one of the soldier Boars from the Realm, a great hairy, tusked pig standing tall on two legs. And dead. He was dead, like the Boars in Rick's dream. A dead soldier Boar from the Golden City, his pig face half rotted away to reveal the skull beneath.

Rick stared up at the tower booth, thunderstruck. The dead Boar peered out at the compound through the glass, grinning its skull grin. Then it lowered its eyes. It looked down. It looked directly at Rick. Its grin grew even wider.

Then it vanished. Melted into air. Gone.

"Did you see that . . . ?" Rick's father began to say.

But Rick was already running past the trees toward the tower.

His mind was racing as he ran. His sneakers smacked the frozen earth as he broke out of the low branches and headed for the tower base. Images from his nightmare rose up before him. The Golden City. The Boar Soldiers coming to life. The skeleton Cobra Guards rising up to bare their fangs. The rotting Harpies swooping down on him from above . . .

Was this a dream too? Was he in a nightmare right now? Or had his nightmares invaded reality?

He reached the base of the tower. He reached the door. He grabbed the handle, pulled it open.

He froze when he saw the rifleman standing just inside. Another Boar?

No, a soldier. Assigned to guard the tower elevator and staircase, the soldier also started in surprise when he saw Rick. He clutched his rifle more tightly, butt and barrel. But his eyes were not afraid. Like everyone else in the compound, he knew Rick. He recognized him.

"What?" he said, confused. "What do you want?"

"There's something wrong in the booth," Rick said breathlessly. "There's someone up there who shouldn't be."

The soldier shook his head, uncertain. "That's impossible. I've been here the whole time. No one could've come in without my seeing them."

Rick didn't wait around to argue. Quickly, he pushed past the guard to the elevator. He pushed the button. The elevator buzzed to life. But the box was up top, in the booth. It started to descend slowly. Rick couldn't wait. He rushed to the stairs.

The stairs wound up above him a long way. Rick had been working out hard for months, bringing his legs back into shape, but they weren't wholly healed. They still hurt when he pushed too far. They hurt now—hurt like fire—as he bounded up the stairs. He was breathing hard by the time he was halfway to the top. He was clinging to the banister, pulling himself onward despite the pain.

Now the booth door appeared before him. He was gasping for breath. The pain lanced through his legs with every step he took. He didn't care. He still had the heart of a football hero, passionate, indomitable. He had woken in agony after some games—lots of games—games in which he'd been tackled hard and driven to the ground again and again. He had woken in agony and gone right back into training. That was who he was. That was what he was like. He was not going to let a little searing physical torture slow him down. He never had before.

He reached the door. He pushed it open. He saw the soldier at once, lying facedown on the floor in a pool of his own blood. The room was filled with a weird smell, not a human smell, a smell like lightning, air on fire, ozone burning.

Rick rushed across the booth to the fallen man. He knelt down beside him. He turned him over.

Dead. A young man, only a little older than Rick. Short, cropped blond hair, blue eyes, open, staring. There was a single wound in his chest. Not a bullet wound. Rick recognized it. He'd seen such wounds before. It was a wound from a sword.

He understood. The man—the soldier—this RL man—had been struck down by a soldier Boar—a creature from the Realm.

But how?

Rick knelt there staring into the soldier's staring dead eyes.

Is this a dream?

It wasn't. He knew it wasn't.

What is going on? he thought. *What in the world is happening?*

LEVEL TWO:
BABA YAGA'S TABLE

6. CONTRACT KILLER

HAROLD HEPPLEWHITE, A professional mur-
derer, stepped out of his car into a ghost town. Not long
ago—not long ago at all—this had been a working facility,
a secret high-tech outpost surrounded by an enclosure that
was almost the dark mirror image of the MindWar compound: barbed wire, guard towers, soldiers with machine
guns standing watch.

This, however, was Kurodar's headquarters, a secret
station hidden in deep jungle on a deserted island off the
coast of Africa. This was where the Realm was created,
where it sprang out of the terrorist's imagination and
spread through cyberspace.

Hepplewhite looked around him. The once busy compound was all but abandoned now. The barracks were dark
and empty. Windows broken. Doors banging in slowly
rising wind. The soldiers were gone, the guard towers
unmanned. Only a few local men and women wandered
here and there. South African natives from poverty-
stricken villages, they had been shipped over to the island
to do the outpost's cooking and cleaning. Hepplewhite

spotted one of them—a very dark-skinned woman in khaki rags—carrying a pot of some sort of steaming food across the empty area to the large building at the center of the place.

It was an odd building, this central one. A white, modern, faceless tower without windows. To Hepplewhite, it looked less like a building than some kind of bizarre machine. But there was a door set in the ground floor. As he watched, the woman with the pot disappeared through it.

Hepplewhite left his car behind and headed after her.

Harold Hepplewhite was a slender man of medium height with the narrow, intelligent face of a librarian. Oily black hair, slicked back. Mild eyes blinking behind round wire-rimmed glasses. Thin lips decorated with an even thinner mustache. He wore white linen pants and a white linen jacket over a paisley shirt open at the throat. He didn't look at all like the sort of man who would kill you, but in fact he would kill you without hesitation and never think much about it afterward. He had murdered people with guns, knives, garrotes, and other assorted tools too gruesome to mention. He'd even shot a guy with an arrow once. He was not a freelancer. This was his steady job. The Axis Assembly kept him on retainer, and he was always ready to go to work. When someone became a problem for the Assembly, it was Hepplewhite's job to make him stop being a problem—in other words, to make him dead.

Now it was Kurodar who had become a problem for the Assembly and Hepplewhite's assignment was to deal with him—which was to say, kill him.

Hepplewhite reached inside his jacket. His hand brushed the butt of the pistol in the holster under his arm. It was a custom-made .22 with a built-in sound suppressor. It fired almost silently, and its small bullets were hollow and contained a poison that would kill a man almost instantly if the bullet itself didn't do the job. But Hepplewhite did not draw the weapon. Instead he reached for the smart phone in his shirt pocket. He drew it out. Pressed one button. Spoke two words: "I'm here." And slipped the phone back into his shirt.

Then he put his hands in the pockets of his slacks and began to stroll slowly across the compound toward the white building. He glanced around casually as he walked, but there was nothing to worry about that he could see. There were no gunmen, no guards. They had all run away the moment they heard the Assembly was abandoning the MindWar Project. They all knew what that meant. They all knew what would come next: Harold Hepplewhite. And Death.

With no one to stop him or question him, Hepplewhite reached the door of the building, pulled it open, and went inside.

It was downright eerie in here. An enormous lobby like the lobby on the ground floor of a New York City office tower. But no one around. No one at all. No noise. No motion. An empty chair behind the reception desk. No lights on. The security terminals all dark.

Hepplewhite's footsteps echoed on the tiled floor, ghostly, as he passed through.

The elevator wasn't working, but the door to the stairwell was ajar. As he stood at the top of the stairwell, Hepplewhite could hear the footsteps of the woman with the food descending to the bottom. Still moving slowly and casually, he followed her down.

At the foot of the stairs, he came into a long corridor with fluorescent lights in the ceiling. Some of the lights were off, some were on, some were blinking fitfully, blue glare and shadows alternating on the floor below. Hands in his pants pockets, Hepplewhite passed beneath them. He passed several guard stations, but there were no guards. He went through several heavy iron doors, but they were all unlocked and standing open. Whenever he paused and listened, he could hear the woman's footsteps echoing up ahead of him.

At last, he turned a corner and caught sight of her again. She was entering the final room, Kurodar's room, the Control Room, the place where the Realm was made.

The woman had just gone through the door. Hepplewhite went after her. He reached the threshold. He stepped over.

And he nearly gagged at what he saw.

The brilliant physicist Ivan Doshenko—the terrorist now known as Kurodar—had always been an ugly little man. Stoop-shouldered and small, he had always had a face like a skull crossed with a toad. But now . . . now, the man was an atrocity. A slimy purple barely human thing strapped to a chair, wires and tubes going in and out of him blending seamlessly with sinews and nerves and veins. His body and the banks of computers all around him were so completely linked that Hepplewhite found it difficult to distinguish the man from the machine.

Disgusting, Hepplewhite thought. *Killing him will just put him out of his misery.* Not that he cared whether Kurodar was miserable or not.

The woman with the pot of food stood beside the creature, spooning soup into the toothless hole of his mouth. Two other men, also South African villagers, also dressed in old khaki, stood tending the machines and screens that blinked and fizzled all around the room. They glanced over at Hepplewhite when he entered, then quickly glanced away. Their eyes were wide and frightened. They had been expecting him and only hoped he would leave them alive after dispatching Kurodar. He would. He did not kill for pleasure, after all. It was just a business to him.

Kurodar's huge, insanely bloodshot eyes also turned in Hepplewhite's direction. If the scientist felt fear, he didn't show it. He merely lifted one withered branch of an arm and made a gesture, brushing the woman away. She withdrew, taking her food with her and, with a quick, frightened backward glance, hurried out of the room.

"Hepplewhite," said Kurodar. Whatever his voice had once been like, it was now a dead echoing thing. It sounded like something dropped into a deep well. His Russian accent was still thick, and the loss of his teeth and the atrophy of his lips made his words indistinct. "Have a seat," he said.

But Hepplewhite remained standing, slouched, his hands in his pockets. "No need," he said. "I won't be here long."

Kurodar's laughter sounded like a big hollow gong being struck repeatedly. "You mean simply to kill me and be on your way?" he said in a more or less pleasant tone.

Hepplewhite shrugged. "You know how it is. You are a loose end. Loose ends must be tied up." The sight of Kurodar disgusted him, but he forced himself to look into the red-streaked eyes. There was an intensity of feeling in them, but what feeling? Hepplewhite wasn't sure. "You don't seem to be afraid," he said.

Kurodar laughed again. "Of you? No."

"Of death then. Are you at peace with death?"

Kurodar stopped laughing suddenly. Suddenly his tone was dark and seething. "I am at peace with nothing," he said. "I wake up in a rage every morning and go to sleep in a rage every night. Between waking and sleeping, I think of one thing only: vengeance, nothing but vengeance. I am never at peace."

Hepplewhite nodded. His handlers at the Assembly had briefed him on Kurodar. He knew what the terrorist said of himself was true. Doshenko had been the son of a high-ranking KGB official in the old slave state of the Soviet Union. The KGB was the brutal Soviet security agency—their spies and secret police. Kurodar's father, Adam Doshenko, had had enormous power. With a single word and for no apparent reason, he could have almost anyone thrown in prison, order him tortured, order him killed. Kurodar's father could make his enemies disappear forever with a fingersnap—and he often did.

When the Soviet Union collapsed, a mob had dragged Kurodar's father out into the street. In their fury at a lifetime of oppression, they had beaten the man to death right in front of his son's eyes. Kurodar had worshipped his father, and the killing had marked him for life. He had nursed his anger inside him until it grew into a titanic and obsessional rage.

He wanted vengeance—not on the people who had mobbed and beaten his father. He wanted vengeance on America. The Americans were the ones he blamed. It was the Americans more than anyone who had hemmed in the U.S.S.R. and brought her down, all without firing a single shot. And why? As Kurodar saw it, all his father wanted— all the Soviets wanted—was to make all people equal. That's why they had killed tens of millions of their citizens. That's why they had conquered hundreds of millions more. What else could they do? People were not naturally equal. You had to make them so! Cut them all down to the same size and kill the ones who refused to go along.

Wasn't equality worth it? Of course it was. Equality was only fair, after all!

But the Americans hadn't seen it that way. No, they had destroyed his country and caused the murder of his father, and Kurodar had sworn vengeance on all of them. As Hepplewhite understood it, that's what this whole crazy MindWar Realm scheme was all about. Payback. Bring America down.

A fantasy, Hepplewhite thought. That's all it was. However brilliant he might be, Kurodar was just an angry little geek with a pipe dream of revenge. The Axis Assembly also wanted America destroyed, after all, but they were willing to do it the right way, slowly, almost unnoticeably, day by day. Infiltrating their agents into American government where they would preach equality. Placing them in American universities to teach the young about the glories of equality. Getting them jobs in newspapers and on TV . . . until Americans started to cut one another down to size without any need for violent intervention at all.

But the Assemblymen had allowed Kurodar to seduce them with his daydreams of a United States in flames. The MindWar Realm. Madness.

Now Kurodar's grand schemes had been foiled—twice—and by a kid who played video games. Enough. It was time to bring this madness to an end.

"Well," Hepplewhite said drily. "You will have peace now. I have come to give you peace."

He took his right hand from his pocket and was about

to reach inside his jacket for the .22 under his arm. But when Kurodar spoke again, something in his tone made Hepplewhite pause.

"You have a smart phone in your shirt pocket, do you not?" he said.

Hepplewhite's hand hung in the air. His eyes narrowed in confusion. "Excuse me?"

"A phone. In your pocket," said the slimy purple thing that had once been a genius.

Hepplewhite shrugged. "So?"

"So I have entered it."

Hepplewhite did not understand. Entered his phone? What did that mean? He knew he should just shoot the man and get it over with. But he was curious. "Entered . . . ?" he began to say.

"The phone. It's a computer after all. I have linked my mind to it through the MindWar Realm. I have taken it over."

"Ah," said Hepplewhite. *This is nonsense*, he thought. Once again, he started to reach for the gun beneath his jacket.

But Kurodar said, "If you put your hand inside your jacket, I will cause your phone to explode with a force that will embed a thousand shards of plastic in your heart. You will be dead before your gun ever clears the holster."

Hepplewhite's face went blank. His hand froze midway to his jacket. He became very aware of the screens and machines blinking in the room all around him, the machines whose wires ran into Kurodar's veins and nerve endings as if he and they were one. "No," he said. "If you could do that, you'd have killed the Traveler and his kid—what's his name . . . Rick Dial—by now."

"The Traveler's defenses are deep and strong. Yours aren't."

Hepplewhite shook his head slowly. "I don't believe you," he said—but he did not continue to reach for his gun.

Kurodar laughed again, *boom, boom, boom*, that dull drumming noise. "You believe me, all right. And here is what you are going to do now. You are going to leave here. You are going to return to your friends in the Assembly. You are going to tell them I want nothing from them. I need nothing from them. I am going to destroy the MindWar Project and I'm going to destroy the United States of America, and I need no one to help me."

Hepplewhite's hand still hovered near his gun. He was not sure what to think. He was not sure what to believe. He was not sure what to do. He said, "What makes you think you'll succeed this time? The Traveler and his boy have defeated you at every turn."

"Yes," said Kurodar. "But this time I have a secret weapon."

"What's that?" said Hepplewhite.

"Rick Dial himself," said Kurodar.

And with that, the terrorist began to laugh again, a great booming laugh that caused him to throw his head back against his seat.

And Hepplewhite thought, *Now!* Like a flash, while Kurodar was fully distracted, the assassin's hand went inside his jacket and grabbed his gun.

A second later, Harold Hepplewhite was lying on the floor on his back, his eyes staring up at the ceiling through the round lenses of his glasses, his paisley shirt soaked with blood, his white jacket beginning to turn red, his heart shredded by the shrapnel from his exploded phone.

The two men who were tending Kurodar's machines—the two villagers from the continent—stood staring at the dead assassin with wide eyes.

"Take him out of here and bury him," said Kurodar quietly.

7. MOONLIT GROVE

RICK DREADED THE darkness. He dreaded sleep. Would his nightmares return? Would they take him back into the Realm again? Would they take him back to the Golden City and its living-dead creatures, Boars and Cobras and Harpies?

Were his dreams even dreams at all? Or were they some strange new form of reality? Was reality itself even real anymore?

Who could you trust if you couldn't trust yourself? If you couldn't trust your own mind?

Rick didn't know. He only knew he was afraid. Of the night. Of the dark. Of sleep and dreams.

He tried not to show his fear to the others. They were all sitting together in the Dials' living room. Raider had been sent upstairs to bed half an hour ago. But Rick and his mother and father and Molly and Professor Jameson remained. The scene was bizarrely normal. The Christmas tree stood in the corner, its crown scraping the ceiling, its branches hung with ornaments and lights. A fire was crackling happily in the fireplace. Rick's mother had put some Christmas music on the Sonos—Mom loved Christmas music and played it every chance she got. Right this minute, "Adeste Fideles" was sounding softly in the background.

And they were talking about the murdered guard.

That's what made the normalcy so weird. In that homey Christmas setting, the conversation seemed like something from another planet, as if an alien language had been dubbed in over an ordinary family scene.

Outside, on the compound grounds, things were not normal at all. Ever since the guard had been found dead in the tower booth, everyone had been on edge. Commander Mars had ordered the entire area searched. The guard who had been assigned to the base of the tower was in custody and under suspicion. Miss Ferris had subjected Rick to a sharp interrogation about the incident, as if he were also a suspect, even though the Traveler had been with him the whole time. Even now, after nightfall, there were flashlight beams crisscrossing the darkness out there as guards went over the area yet again.

"You're sure you saw the Boar?" Professor Jameson asked Rick one more time.

"We both saw it," said the Traveler. "It was there."

"And not just a Boar Soldier," said Rick. "A dead one. His face all rotted."

"Ew!" said Molly.

"But how is that possible?" Professor Jameson asked.

Both Rick and his father shook their heads.

"How do I dream about battles and wake up with scratches?" said Rick. "None of it makes any sense."

"Oh, I'm pretty sure it makes sense," the Traveler corrected him gently. "We just don't understand the sense it makes. Not yet, anyway."

They were all speaking in low voices. Partly, that was so Raider wouldn't hear them upstairs. But partly, too, it was because they did not want anyone outside to hear them either. No one would say it out loud, but the truth was they didn't trust anyone outside of their little circle. Like Victor One, they were all convinced there was a traitor within the project. Mars, Miss Ferris, even the Traveler's old friend Leila Kent . . . Any one of them could be the turncoat in their midst. That's why they had not told anyone about the Boar. Rick and his father had made this decision together. Mars was already angry and suspicious, threatening to ban Rick from the Realm. An incident like this would only make things worse. So for now, they allowed the death of the soldier in the guard tower to remain a mystery.

"I'm worried that it has something to do with me," said Rick suddenly. They all turned to look at him. He dropped his eyes and stared at the floor. "Maybe what Mars says is true. Maybe when I went through the Breach, I caused . . . I don't know . . . some kind of disturbance . . ."

"Is that possible?" This was Molly, looking now from one face to another, from Rick to her father to Rick's father to Rick again. "I mean, how could that have anything to do with a Realm creature coming into reality? How is that even possible?"

The Traveler's eyebrows went up over the top rims of his spectacles. He didn't answer. No one said anything for a long time. There was hardly a sound besides a choir softly singing "O Holy Night."

"Well . . . ," said Professor Jameson finally.

He and Molly got up to go. They were leaving the compound tomorrow. They had been brought here to keep them safe from Kurodar's men—and the Traveler had seized the opportunity to get Professor Jameson to help him with his work. But since the guard's murder, Mars had declared that only necessary personnel would be allowed on the grounds. He had arranged to have a transport truck come and pick up the professor and his daughter and take them back to Putnam Hills. He would have them watched by security guards from now on to keep them safe.

Rick's father and mother walked them to the door. Rick went outside with them into the biting cold. Professor Jameson walked off to their barracks, leaving Molly and Rick alone in the night. They stood together near where Rick and his father had stood, near the little grove of trees outside the house. A half-moon had risen over the compound. Its silver light turned the winter branches into spiral patterns against the sky. Flashlight beams were visible here and there as guards patrolled the night. And above them, in the tower, Rick could make out the shadow of a new guard, pacing.

Rick and Molly stood close together in the darkness. Rick could see his old friend's eyes glistening in the moonlight. He could smell her scent. Her nearness made his heart hurt. There were so many things he wanted to say to her, but he couldn't find the right words for any of them. It wasn't like he had some stupid idea of ever getting romantic with her again. That was over; it was too late to bring those feelings back. He had seen the way Molly looked at Victor One in the hospital room. Something was obviously starting between them, and Rick had no right to interfere with it. V-One was a good man, a soldier, and a hero. He and Molly could make each other very happy.

Rick put his hands in his back pockets. His frosted breath turned silver in the moonlight.

"Well, listen," he said, "I'm gonna miss you around here, but I'm glad you're getting away from all this. Things are getting very weird in old MindWarville, and you'll be a lot better off back at school."

Molly didn't say anything, but Rick could see her nodding in the shadows.

He stumbled on awkwardly. "And listen, you know, you and I have been friends a long time, right? And so I just want you to know that I'm really glad, you know, if you and Victor One . . . what I mean is, V-One's a really good guy and . . . what I'm trying to say . . ."

Molly put her arms around him and kissed him.

It was such a surprise that Rick should have been confused. But he was not confused. He was not anything. He was just kissing her. In fact, he was amazed at how easy it was to find himself doing this, how simple and right it was. He could not understand why he hadn't thought of it before.

Then he held her close to him, his cheek to her cheek, his lips to her ear, her lips to his.

"But . . . I thought you guys, you and Victor One . . . I thought it was you and him now . . . ," Rick whispered.

"That's because you're an idiot," she whispered back. "You don't understand anything."

Rick had to agree. He did not even understand what was happening now. He did not even try.

"There's no one else," Molly said. "There's only you." She drew back from him. She looked at him through the darkness. "Now you're supposed to say that back," she explained to him. "You're supposed to say there's only me."

"There's only you," he said.

"Are you sure?"

Rick hesitated. He thought of Mariel. But in fact he realized that deep down he had always known it was Molly he wanted. "I'm sure," he said. He put his hand against her cheek. His cold hand. Her warm cheek. Molly smiled at him. Then she shivered.

"You better go back to your barracks," he told her. But he didn't want her to go. Inside his house, the darkness was waiting for him. His bed . . . sleep . . . dreams. The Golden City. The living dead. He wished he could stay out here with Molly forever. "Go," he said again.

"All right," she said. She smiled. "I understand. You have to do what you have to do. Go back into the Realm. Destroy the evildoers. Save the world."

"Something like that."

"Just do me one favor, okay?" Molly said. "Don't die. Can you remember that? I mean, even for a dumb jock like you, those are very simple instructions: Do not die."

"How do you spell it?"

"Very funny. I laugh and laugh at your hilarious jokes."

Even in the night, Rick could see the fear in her eyes just as plainly as he could feel the fear inside his own heart. He kissed her one last time. He wrapped his arms around her. "I won't die," he said. "I promise."

He wished he felt sure that he was telling the truth.

8. FEAR EFFECT

THE MOMENT RICK stepped into the house—the moment he saw his mom and dad standing together in the living room, waiting for him—the moment he saw the looks of deep anxiety on their faces—he felt his heart drop so fast, so hard, it was nearly comical, even to him. A few seconds before, out in the brassy cold, he had felt so warm inside, full of Molly's presence and his feelings for her and her feelings for him, that for a few moments everything had seemed simple. Good. Now, here, inside, in the warmth, a chill went through him, making him shudder. It was the chill of fear.

Down the hall, behind the closed door, his room was waiting for him. His bed. Sleep. Those dreams . . .

He stood for another second, looking at the painful worry on his parents' faces. There seemed to be nothing to say.

"I guess I better get to bed," he said. Again, he heard the pale sound of fear in his voice and he hated it.

In his room, he undressed slowly. All the while, he eyed his narrow bed as if it were some kind of prowling animal—an animal that might suddenly leap at him. He pulled some sweatpants on over his scarred legs and worked his way into a T-shirt. Then he just stood there in the center of the room, staring at the bed.

There was a soft knock at the door. His mother came in.

Rick could not get over how different she seemed now that his dad was back. When the Traveler was gone, she had seemed to grow old instantly. She stopped wearing makeup. Her hair got gray and frizzy. Her shoulders started to stoop. Now that Dad was back, it was as if a fresh flood of life and youth had rushed through her. The lines on her face seemed to have disappeared almost magically. She looked wide awake and alert and her eyes were full of light and humor.

The funny thing? She had never lost faith in her husband. He had pretended to run off with an old girlfriend in order to keep the MindWar Project secret and to keep his family safe. But Mom had never believed it, not even for a second. It was Rick who had gotten angry at his dad, Rick who had lost his faith in his father . . . and because of that, had lost his faith in . . . in everything.

Now, as his mom came close to him, he saw her eyes move quickly down to his arm, the scratches on his wrist. Rick flinched. His father had looked at the scratches with cold scientific curiosity, but Rick knew his mom felt a wound in his flesh as if it were a wound in her own. Back in his football days, he had never been sure whether he or she hurt worse after he took a hard sack.

She reached out and gently touched the scabs on his wrist, as if she might have some magical healing power in her fingers. Then she looked up at him quickly, directly into his eyes. "When you were little, I used to sit outside your bedroom door until you could fall asleep," she said with a small smile.

He returned her smile but lopsided, ironic. "I remember. I was scared I would have bad dreams."

"Do you want me to sit outside tonight?"

"I don't think it would help, Ma."

"No. I guess not."

"I guess, in the end," Rick said, "everyone has to go into his dreams alone."

His mother studied his face closely. It made Rick feel weird. Kind of exposed. His mother probably understood him better than anyone else in the world. A lot of times she knew what he was thinking even before he did. When she looked at him closely like that, it felt as if she might be reading his mind. Rick didn't know whether to try to hide from her or just let her see everything. He didn't know if it mattered what he did.

"Did you and Molly work things out?" she asked him.

He snorted. "You saw that coming, huh?"

"My super X-ray future vision."

That actually got a laugh out of him. "It was weird," he said. "After all that worrying, trying to find the answer, the answer was right there. It was so easy."

"Funny how that works," Mom said.

He went on smiling at the memory another moment: he and Molly among the moonlit trees. Then he stopped smiling. He met his mom's steady gaze. The words seemed to come out of him on their own, without his will. "I'm scared, Mom," he said.

She nodded.

"I'm scared something's wrong with me. Because of the Realm. The Breach. I'm scared something's wrong with my brain. I mean, I'm not afraid of Kurodar. I'm not afraid of his monsters or his men. Or that is, I am afraid, sure I am, but it doesn't bother me. You know? When it comes down to it, I'll fight them. I'll fight anybody."

His mom nodded. "I know you will."

"But when you can't trust your own brain . . ."

For the first time tonight, his mother's eyes widened a little in alarm. "No, don't do that. Don't trust your own brain, Rick."

"What do you mean? Why not?"

"Because. Because your brain can steer you wrong, that's why. If you want to do the stupidest, ugliest, meanest thing in the world, your brain'll come up with excuses for you to do it. You know it will. It happens to everyone. Everyone who ever cheated on a test or hurt a friend or stuck a needle in his arm or got behind the wheel of a car when he was drunk—they all thought they had perfectly good reasons to do it. Their brains told them so. You can never trust your brain."

Her words surprised him at first, but when he thought

about it, he knew she was right. He could think of half a dozen times off the top of his head when he had done something really, really stupid and his brain had said to him, *Great idea, Champ! You ride that skateboard down the steepest hill in town two days before training begins! Sure thing. What could go wrong?*

"But if I can't trust my own brain . . . ," he began.

"Remember when you were angry with your father?" his mother said—and it was as if she had read his mind, as if she knew he'd just been thinking about that. "Remember when you thought he'd left us to go off with Leila Kent? You didn't just get angry at Dad, did you?"

Rick shrugged. "I guess not. I got angry at everything. I got angry at God. Dad believed in God so much and then he left—I thought he left . . . So I got angry."

"What do you think about your father now?" she asked him.

Rick opened his mouth to answer, but no words came out. He was thinking about the last time he was in the Realm, when he was in the fighter craft doing battle against the Octo-Guardian in the midst of the living blackness of MindWar space. He had been forced to make a choice, forced to decide whether to stop Kurodar's attack on Washington, DC, or to rush through the Breach and rescue Molly and Victor One right away. It was only then, only in that moment, that he had begun to understand what kind of choice his dad had had to make when he left home, what kind of sacrifice he had been willing to make out of love . . .

"I'm not angry at him anymore," he said. "I get it now."

His mom reached up and pushed his hair back off his forehead. "You won't go into your dreams alone," she told him. "You'll never go anywhere alone. I promise."

When his mother was gone, Rick stood another long moment looking down at his bed. There was still a weight of fear lying at the pit of his stomach. But he couldn't stay awake forever. He pulled back the covers and lay down.

He reached up and switched off the light on the wall above him. He lay in the dark. For a long time, he did not dare to close his eyes. The silver moonlight came through the edges of the curtains. Now and then one of the flashlights of the patrolling soldiers played its beam across the back of the fabric.

You won't go into your dreams alone.

Rick's thoughts returned to Molly. Her eyes gleaming in the shadows. Her lips on his . . . A simple answer to what had seemed an almost impossibly complicated question. An answer that had been there all along, waiting for him to find it.

You'll never go anywhere alone.

Rick let his eyes sink slowly shut.

Never alone, he thought.

Moments later, he fell asleep—and the horror began.

9. BLAST 'EM

THE ETERNAL BLACKNESS swept up out of the sarcophagus and seized the living Rick by the throat. At the same moment, Favian let out a terrified scream. The door to the church burst open and the dead swarmed in.

It was a hellish scene. The darkness was swarming over him, choking him, swallowing him, threatening to pull him down into some nightmare without end. And the church, this strange, colorful church full of beautiful mosaics, was suddenly swarming with screeching Harpies, slithering Cobras, charging Boars, their bodies and faces half rotten with death, their skull-heads grinning as they charged across the nave to kill him.

Rick couldn't breathe. The edges of his vision were falling into shadow. He sensed the dead creatures of the Golden City storming across the church floor, through the church air. They were nearly on him, about to destroy him.

Then—*flash*—a blast of blue light.

Favian. Standing beside him. His eyes so wide with fear that you would have thought he would be running away as fast as he could. But—typical Favian—scared as he was, he was not running anywhere. He had gathered the diminishing energy inside him and sent it zigzagging out of his outstretched hand like lightning.

The blast smacked against the darkness and drove it back—away from Rick, down into the coffin. Horribly, Rick felt the blow as if it had hit him too. As the darkness sank away from him, he staggered backward, his mind reeling. He let out a hoarse gasp and dragged in a fresh breath of air.

"Rick, behind you!"

He didn't need Favian's warning cry. He knew what was coming.

He spun round, Mariel's sword gripped in his hand. He faced the swarming dead.

His vision was filled with the screaming skull of a rotten Harpy. It was sweeping down out of the high church shadows, its long talons swiping at Rick's face.

There was a loud metallic sting as Rick raised his sword and blocked the talons with its silver blade. Then he turned and swung the weapon almost like a baseball bat, sending the Harpy pinwheeling through the air. He didn't wait to see where it landed and swung the sword back just in time to block the thrusting open mouth of a half-rotted Cobra Guard. The sword's blow removed the Cobra's head, and the beast dissolved in a snap-and-fizzle of purple light.

With the same motion, Rick raised the sword above his own head crosswise. The horizontal blade caught the powerful downward blow of a Boar's sword. Dead Boar and living man froze like that together, sword to sword. Dead though he was, the Boar was strong. He was trying to force his blade down through Rick's skull by sheer muscle power.

Rick lifted his foot and kicked the Boar in his putrid stomach as hard as he could. The Boar went flying backward, knocking over two other Boars as if they were pins in a bowling alley.

"There are too many, Rick!" Favian shouted. "Run!"

Rick could hear the panic in the blue man's high-pitched cry, but all the same, he knew the sprite was right. They had no chance against this mob of creature corpses. They had to get out of here.

Rick glanced over at the large coffin in the center of the nave. The darkness was bubbling and seething in there, as if it were preparing to leap up again and seize him.

And the waves of dead creatures kept pouring toward him.

"This way," Favian cried.

Favian had a big advantage in these run-for-your-life situations. He didn't have to run. He just flashed away like a streak of light. A single second—a single line of glowing blue—and he was no longer standing beside Rick at the coffin but was instead at a door in the back of the church. It was a great heavy wooden door with iron reinforcements. Favian was using both hands and all his might to drag it open.

Mariel had taught Rick that he could manipulate the Realm's reality. With enough focus and concentration, he could bring the power of his spirit to bear and actually change the shape of things in MindWar. Not only could he turn himself into the shapes of the various monsters he saw—for a brief period, anyway—but if he really worked at it, really brought his old quarterback focus to the game, he could even occasionally flash like Favian too.

What else might he be able to do?

He didn't know. But this would be an excellent time to find out.

Because now he was surrounded. The dead creatures had spread out around him in a circle and were now closing that circle like a noose. Cobra fangs darted at him, Harpy talons slashed, and Boar swords jabbed, each looking to slip a strike in past Mariel's flashing sword. Where the large sarcophagus blocked the dead's advance, the darkness within was beginning to surge and rise and lick at the edges of the box. Even if Rick could focus his mind enough to flash away, there was nowhere to flash to. He had to think of something else.

"Rick! Come on!" Favian shouted. He had the heavy door fully open now. But there was just no way for Rick to get to him.

Rick turned in every direction. On every side, the screaming creatures closed in.

A thought came to him.

In video games, as your character advances, he acquires

powers and weapons along the way. You might start out with just the Blade of Nastiness, say, but pretty soon, if you kill enough monsters, you acquire the Fire Sword of Genuine Incredibleness and then the Lightning Sword of Really Cool Headsplitting Greatness until finally you have the most powerful weapon of all, the Death Blade of All-Around Awesomeness . . . or whatever.

This same thing had happened to Rick here in the MindWar Realm. When he had first met Mariel, she had given him a sort of rusty iron sword that he could just barely thrust through the body of the wounded Spider-Snake. But by the time he had to do real, desperate battle against Kurodar's security forces, she had coated the sword in steel, strengthening its blade and perfecting its design until it was a master weapon he could wield against the Realm's most powerful security bots.

But weapons weren't the only thing that got better in a video game. There were also powers—they also got upgraded as you went along. And that also happened here in MindWar. In his first trips into the Realm, Rick had used his concentration to turn himself into the likeness of one of the Alligator Guards who patrolled Kurodar's forces. Later, he could not only take the shape of a soldier Boar, but, if he focused well enough, he could even sometimes flash around like Favian.

So if the video-game analogy continued . . .

As the dead Harpies and Cobras and Boars closed in on him, slashing with claws and fangs and swords, closer and closer to tearing him to pieces, Rick shifted his focus to the silver blade of Mariel's sword. Maybe if he could charge it with the energy of his spirit . . .

It was hard—so hard—to focus with that horde of death-dealing monsters closing in on him. But then, as a quarterback, he'd often had to focus with a horde of three-hundred-pound linemen thundering at him, so . . . he recalled that experience. He steadied his mind. He steadied his heart. He focused his spirit on the blade.

Almost immediately, the blade began to glow, and then glow brighter. It surrounded itself with a nimbus of bright yellow light. Rick focused hard and the metal of the sword actually began to pulse and throb with his inner energy.

A Harpy shrieked and dove at him out of the sky.

Do it! Rick thought.

He released the energy of the sword. It was like setting off an explosion. The spirit energy he had pumped into the sword burst out of it. The yellow glow flashed white, expanding in one great and sudden blast.

The dead creatures never saw it coming. They were all charging, closing, striking when the blast hit. It caught them mid-attack and hurled them backward. The Harpy that was in the midst of dropping down on top of him was thrown upward, sailing all the way to the church ceiling, where it smacked into a mosaic and then dropped down *thunk* at Rick's feet like a stone. The other monsters—Boars and Harpies and Cobras, all of them—went tumbling into one another, some dropping to the mosaic floor, others stumbling on their heels, their arms pinwheeling for balance.

But Rick never lost his focus, not for a moment. He never stopped working the Realm with his spirit. The moment the ring of monsters was blown back, he dissolved himself into a Favian-like flash and streaked away. A split second later, he was standing beside his blue friend at the open door at the rear of the church.

"That was AMAZING!" Favian cried out with wild excitement. "That was . . . that was . . ."

"Tell me what it was later," said Rick. "Now, let's bounce!"

"Oh, right, smart idea," said Favian—and good thing, too, because even now some of the dead were clambering to get their balance back, coming out of their dazes and getting ready to renew their attack.

In a dazzling blue streak, Favian flashed through the doorway, leaving the heavy door to start swinging shut behind him.

The effort of focusing his spirit had worn Rick out. He had no more flash in him. He grabbed the door with one hand to hold it open. Then he slipped through into the shadows beyond.

He found himself standing on the top landing of a spiral staircase of heavy stone steps. The blue glow of Favian was receding around the spiral, out of sight.

Rick found a large wooden plank leaning against the

wall in here. Obviously, it was meant to rest in the door-frame holders and keep the door barred.

Rick set his sword aside, hoisted the plank across the door, and set it in place. *That ought to hold the dead for a little while,* he thought.

Then he grabbed his sword and went running after his friend.

10. WITCH'S WORKSHOP

RICK AND FAVIAN hurried down the winding stairs. They were surrounded by deep shadows. Only a low blue glow emanating from Favian's palm lit their descent. Holding his sword in one hand, Rick reached out with the other to steady himself against the wall. He felt the pebbly mosaic there under his fingertips. Now and then, when Favian's glow hit the wall just right, Rick caught a glimpse of some mosaic face staring at him. He knew these were the faces of saints and apostles, but they didn't look very saintly or holy. They just seemed grim, condemnatory, and basically kind of spooky.

Favian flashed ahead only a little at a time. He didn't want to leave Rick in utter blackness. Also, he was scared to be alone in this place. He would zip down a couple of steps and then wait to allow Rick to catch up and then flash away again.

"Where are we going?" Rick said breathlessly.

"I was just going to ask you the same question," said Favian, flashing away.

Rick caught up with him and said, "I don't even know

how I got here in the first place. I don't remember coming through the portal into the Realm. I'm thinking maybe this is just a dream."

"Well, I hope not. If it is, then I'm just a dream too," said Favian, and he flashed around the curve of the spiral stairs out of sight.

Rick turned the corner and the sprite came into view again. "You're not a dream," said Rick. And then he remembered something else: "You're an Army clerk named Fabian Child."

Favian looked like he was about to flash away again, but Rick's words stopped him. "Wait, what? I'm who? What?"

"An Army . . ."

"Clerk. Yes. That's right!" Favian's eyes grew bright as the memories flooded back to him. "My dad wanted me to be a soldier! Like he was. So I joined the military, but instead of sending me into any war zones, they just put me in an office because I knew how to use a computer. Which was fine with me. I was never much good at fighting except in . . ."

". . . video games," said Rick.

Just then, there was a loud bang above them. The dead had found the stairwell door and were pounding against it, trying to break through.

"It's all coming back to me," said Favian softly. "I joined the military so I could show my dad I wasn't a coward. The only problem is I actually *am* a coward!"

Another bang from above. Rick looked over his shoulder, up the stairs. They had to get out of here before the dead broke through.

"You're no coward," Rick said quickly. "You're just a nervous type of guy. That's all. You've got courage to burn when you need it. But you know what? There are times when acting like a coward is the smart move."

"Really? Like when?"

"Like now. We've gotta get out of here."

"Oh . . . oh, right . . ." But Favian paused for one more second and murmured almost in wonder: "An Army clerk who played video games. I remember." Rick could make out his friend's glowing face only dimly, but he could see, even in the shadows, that the guy was delighted to have his identity back after all this time.

Then Favian flashed away, and Rick continued down the spiral stairs after him.

Rick came around another curve. The pounding of the dead against the door echoed above them. Favian was ready to flash away . . .

"Wait. Stop. Look," said Rick.

The two stood together and stared down into the shadows.

There was a faint line of light off to one side.

"A door, I think," said Rick.

"An exit maybe," said Favian hopefully.

"But an exit to where?" said Rick.

"Right," said Favian, not so hopefully.

Rick continued his descent toward the light—and Favian (who really could be sort of a coward sometimes) let him go ahead, hanging back fearfully behind him. Every now and then, the blue sprite would flash forward to catch up, but never so far forward that he got in front of Rick. So it was Rick who reached the dim light first.

He found a platform just off the stairs, and yes, sure enough, there was a door. Rick moved close to it, listening for any noises that might let him know what was behind it. After a few seconds, he heard something. It sounded like . . . what? . . . a high-pitched cackling laugh.

"What is that?" Favian breathed in his ear. He had come flashing up stealthily behind him again.

Rick shook his head. "Sounds like an old woman . . ."

"Like a witch, you mean," said Favian. "Like a witch in one of those fairy tales who lures you into her lair then cooks and eats you."

Rick gave him a look: Favian would think of something scary like that. It wasn't helpful. And even worse, it was kind of true. It did sound like there was a cackling witch behind the door.

The cackling came again—but it was almost immediately drowned out by a fresh series of echoing bangs from the door upstairs. The pounding was accompanied by a noise like wood splintering. The plank that Rick had used to bar the door was beginning to give way. Another few tries and the dead monsters would break through the door and come pouring down the spiral stairs like a flood of . . . well, like a flood of dead monsters.

Rick glanced quickly down the stairs. Nothing he could see down there but more blackness. There was no choice. He reached for the door.

"What are you doing?" said Favian. "We could get lured in and cooked and eaten."

"Maybe," said Rick. In this crazy place, he wasn't sure Favian was wrong. "But we've gotta try it. We've got nowhere else to go."

He reached out and pushed the big door. It creaked as it swung open like a door in a ghost house. The dim light grew brighter and spilled out onto the platform where Rick and Favian were standing. The door swung open farther and they saw where the light was coming from.

"Whoa!" said Favian. His amazement almost overcame his fear.

Rick didn't blame him. He was also amazed. He felt the breath come streaming out of him as he stared into the light.

Through the door was a cramped room with a low ceiling. There were no mosaics here, only naked wood. The room was windowless and empty . . .

Empty, that is, except for the witch and her crystal table.

She sure looked like a witch, anyway. In fact, she looked almost exactly like a witch from a storybook or cartoon. She had greenish skin and thick white hair that fell heavily out of the red bandanna tied around her forehead. Her face was deeply wrinkled and spotted with thick warts. Her nose was warty, too, and sharp and bent. Her grinning mouth was almost toothless. And her pale eyes, despite the grin on her mouth, were full of malevolence. She actually did look like the sort of creature who would cook and eat children.

The witch went on cackling, moving her hands in mystic gestures over the table in front of her. It was the table that was giving off the light. It was a round table made of some sort of clear, crystal-like material. It looked almost like a gigantic diamond. The white light was coming out of it from who knew where. It was shining brighter and then dimmer in a pulsing rhythm. The light rose and bathed the witch's face and made her look more terrible still. It spread across the room, striking the heavy ceiling beams above and throwing black shadows across the floor below.

The witch continued to gaze into the light. She did not look up at Rick and Favian. But after a moment, as they stood in the doorway gaping at her, she beckoned them with a rolling motion of one stick-like finger.

"Come in, come in, boys, and meet Baba Yaga," she said in a high witchy singsong. "She'll show you visions of what has been and what will be—and all will become clear to you."

Rick and Favian glanced at each other. They heard

more pounding and splintering from the door upstairs. Rick shrugged. Might as well get killed and eaten by a witch as by a raving swarm of half-decayed monsters. He stepped into the room. Favian followed. Rick pushed the door shut behind him, hoping the dead monsters would pass down the spiral stairs without noticing it was there.

"Oh, don't worry. They can't reach you here," said the witch, as if reading Rick's mind. "Baba Yaga's room is the one room in the Golden City that no one can enter."

"But . . . but we just did enter it," said Favian nervously.

For the first time, the witch—this Baba Yaga—lifted her face to them and caught them in the glare of her sinister eyes. "You, yes," she said with another cackle. "Because you're in the Realm but not of it. You are free agents—you and the water woman. The only free agents here. The rest are his creatures."

"Kurodar's?" asked Rick.

But the witch just continued in a low throaty mutter, "Even I'm his creature, poor soul that I am. But he can't touch me. He can't make me leave, much as he may want to."

Rick took another tentative step toward the crystal table. He had to duck under the beam in the ceiling, it was so low. He kept moving. He was curious to see what was in that white light, what exactly the hideous old crone was looking at.

"So," she said with a canny glance up at him, "you want to see what Baba Yaga can show you. The past. The future. Your fate. Come. Come forward. Come and see."

Rick felt Favian's touch—that buzzing, faintly electric touch—on his arm.

"Maybe we shouldn't," Favian whispered. "I'm not sure I want to know my fate. What if it's bad?"

Almost the minute he'd spoken, he let out a gasp as Baba Yaga startled them both with a loud, screeching laugh. "There's a wise lad!" she cried. "Maybe you should listen to him." She cocked a scraggly white eyebrow at Rick. "But you won't, will you, my dear? You're too curious, aren't you? You have to know. You have to know!"

"You said you could show me the past too," said Rick—and he continued to edge toward the crystal table, his feet shuffling along the stone floor almost in spite of himself. "Can you show me how I got here? Can you tell me whether this is real or a dream? Can you tell me if Kurodar . . . ?"

"Come, come, come!" said the witch, making that rolling beckoning gesture with her warty hands again. "Come and see what Baba Yaga can show you."

Rick was nervous—even scared. The old woman's malevolence was so obvious. It was obvious in her eyes . . . in her laugh. It was even obvious in her toothless grin. He didn't trust her. He wasn't sure he should even get this close to her. Maybe she really would grab him and devour him! She sure looked like she might.

But it didn't matter. Baba Yaga was right: He needed to see what she wanted to show him. He needed to know what she knew. How he got here. What was happening. What would happen next.

Favian continued to hang back, but Rick stepped into the white glow surrounding the table. He held his sword down at his side, its tip *screaming* along the floor as he shuffled to the table's edge. He squinted down into the brightness. It was so bright it hurt his eyes, made him squint. He could not see anything but the light coming up out of the core of the crystal.

But the witch said, "Look . . . look . . . ," and once again she passed her bony hands over the surface of the table in weird, flowing patterns. As she did, the light began to grow softer. It seemed to spread out under Rick, almost as if it were drifting apart like clouds. Rick felt like he was falling, falling into the misty light. He felt as if it were surrounding him, taking him in. And yes . . . yes, he began to see . . . something . . . images . . . places . . . people . . . inside the light. He couldn't quite make them out . . . He peered down more intently to try to get a better view.

Suddenly, shockingly, the witch seemed to be talking directly into his ear. No, it was more than that. She seemed to be talking and cackling from inside his own head.

"You must go into the belly of the beast, my dear! You must learn what he does not know. You must face the horror he cannot face. Look and see, Rick Dial! Look—and see."

The next thing Rick knew, the images in the crystal table seemed to rise up all around him, surrounding him, closing on him from every side and from above. They were so clear it was almost as if he were truly among them. As if he were one of the images himself.

Rick stared. And now, finally, he saw clearly. The images came into focus, and his eyes went wide with horror. He opened up his mouth to shout in fear, but somehow he couldn't. He couldn't make a noise. He tried to cover his face with his arms. He tried to stop seeing the things he saw. And then . . .

Then he woke up, his face drenched in sweat, his heart hammering. Panting for breath. He sat up, blinking, looking around him.

But what he saw only made his heart hammer harder.

"Where am I?" he gasped.

11.   THE OFFICE

IT HAD BEEN a dream. Another dream. The fight in the church. The flight down the stairs. The witch in her chamber: Baba Yaga. All another dream.

But he was awake now. He was sure of it. He was awake and wearing the sweatpants and T-shirt he'd gone to bed in . . .

Only this—this was not his bedroom.

Where was he? Where was he?

He turned his head, his heart beating hard, his eyes wide. Like Baba Yaga's room, the room around him was small and cramped. Like Baba Yaga's room, this room, too, was bathed in white light. But this was not Baba Yaga's room any more than it was his. The white light was not coming from a crystal table. It was coming from a computer that sat on the desk in front of him. In the glow from the computer, Rick could make out a small, den-like office. There was a Persian rug on the floor, shelves of leather-bound books all around him, the studded leather swivel chair in which he was sitting . . .

He knew this place. He'd been here before. He

remembered it. It was Commander Mars's office, his secret workplace hidden away deep in the underground heart of the MindWar compound. Besides Mars, Rick was the only person who could've gotten in here undetected. Anyone else would have set off every alarm in the compound. But Rick's dad had given him a flash drive that overrode the underground security. Somehow, in his sleep, Rick had used that drive and snuck into this top secret place.

Dazed, Rick looked down at his hand. Sure enough, the override flash drive was gripped in it, his fingers wrapped tightly around it.

Rick shook his head, trying to clear his mind. How had this happened? How had he come here? And why? What was he looking for?

He lifted his eyes to the computer. What was shown on the screen only confused him more. Numbers. Equations. Some sort of specifications. And diagrams of . . . something . . . something that looked like a satellite . . . a disk . . . a cannon emitting a beam of light. Words leapt out at him: "Strike capacity . . . kill zone . . . solar charge . . ." And the title of the page: "SS-317 Battle Station."

It all seemed very important—and very dangerous— but what exactly was it? All this math and diagram stuff . . . He was an athlete, not a scientist. He didn't know how to read this kind of thing.

His brain was swimming. The dream. The witch. Favian. Now this. Was it even real? Was he dreaming still? And if it was real, how . . . ? And why . . . ?

He couldn't figure it out, not any of it. All he knew for sure was that he had to get out of here before someone found him. He didn't want to get into any more trouble with Mars than he was in already.

Rick knew the way back. Into the air vents that piped oxygen through the underground chambers. Back to the compressor room. Up through the vent to the outside. The compressor room was just about the one place in the compound that was rarely guarded for the simple reason that no one could beat the surveillance system that would set off the alarm if you tried to enter. No one, that is, who didn't happen to have the Traveler's flash drive override.

A few minutes later he was out of the underground, out in the night. Pebbles jabbed into the soles of his bare feet as he snuck on tiptoe back to his house. The cold ate through his light clothes, making him shiver. There were soldiers everywhere around him in the darkness, and all of them were tense, watchful, on the lookout for whoever killed the guard in the tower. Several times as Rick hurried across the dirt he had to duck behind a barracks to avoid the flashlight beam of a patrol. Once he even had to hit the ground and hug the side of a latrine barracks, breathing in the sharp stink of ammonia from the toilets inside as a spotlight from one of the towers swept the area.

But finally, he slipped back into his house. It was dark here, quiet. The only light was coming from the Christmas tree, which Mom liked to keep on. Its colored lights spattered the living room with cheerful spots of red and green and blue and yellow and white.

Rick crept past the tree and headed back to his bedroom. He slipped quietly through the door. He lay back down on the bed again.

He lay on his back, his hands behind his head. He figured he would try to think things through as he waited for morning. He wasn't afraid of falling asleep again. He was pretty sure he wasn't going to be able to sleep anymore tonight.

So he lay there and he thought. And three words kept going around and around in his mind. Three words, one question.

What. Just. Happened?

Along with the words, there came images. The dead monsters charging at him horrifically across the church nave. The spiral stairs going down into darkness. The cackling witch and her crystal table. Mars's office . . .

What just happened?

Had any of it been real? It all seemed impossible to him, and impossibly crazy. But he remembered his father's words . . .

I'm pretty sure it makes sense. We just don't understand the sense it makes.

So he told himself: *Think. Work it. Figure it out. Figure out the sense it makes.*

What was it Baba Yaga had told him?

You must go into the belly of the beast. You must learn what he does not know. You must face the horror he cannot face.

He. Kurodar—she must mean Kurodar. You must learn what Kurodar does not know and face the horror Kurodar cannot face. Okay, but how could there be a horror in the Realm that Kurodar couldn't face? The Realm was his place. It was made directly out of his imagination. It came straight out of his own brain . . .

Which reminded him of what his mother had said.

Don't trust your own brain, Rick. Your brain can steer you wrong.

Maybe that's what Baba Yaga was talking about. Maybe there was something in Kurodar's brain—and therefore something in the Realm—that Kurodar couldn't trust. Something that frightened him.

He can't make me leave, much as he may want to.

Those were Baba Yaga's words.

Even I'm his creature, poor soul that I am. But he can't touch me. That's what she said. *He can't make me leave . . .*

Lying on his bed, his hands behind his head, Rick blinked up at the ceiling. He was feeling tired now, worn out by the night's insane adventure. But oddly enough, as his mind began to grow fatigued, his thoughts began to flow more smoothly.

And it occurred to him: His dad was right. There really was some sort of sense to all this when you thought about it.

The Golden City was the source and battery of the MindWar Realm. It was the interface where Kurodar's mind linked with his computers and sent out the energy and images that created the red plains and the blue forests and the yellow sky that served as pathways into American computer systems. The security bots, the fortresses, the airships—everything in the Realm came out of Kurodar's mind by way of the Golden City.

So what if there were things in there—in Kurodar's mind—that he didn't want to have in there. Things he wished he could get rid of but could not.

Don't trust your own brain.

He can't make me leave, much as he may want to.

You must face the horror he cannot face.

Maybe the images in Baba Yaga's crystal table were part of this horror Kurodar couldn't get rid of. Maybe this was the horror Rick had to face.

So what was it? What were the images?

He had seen them. In the dream. He remembered. Baba Yaga had opened the vision of the table to him and he had stepped inside. What was there?

His mind began to drift backward as he tried to remember what had awakened him from his sleep in such terror. He tried to recall those images . . .

Then, suddenly, it was morning.

Startled, Rick realized he had fallen back to sleep. His mouth was dry. His head was muzzy. He couldn't remember what he'd been thinking about. What was it . . . ?

But before he could even start to look for the answer, there was a sharp knock at his door. The door came open and his father was there.

"Get dressed, son," he said. "They need us. Let's go."

12. TRACE MEMORY

A LIGHT SNOW had fallen during the last watches of the night. The ground of the MindWar compound was covered by a patina of white that was already melting in the pale early morning sun. As Rick and his father walked across the open space shoulder to shoulder, Rick filled his dad in on what had happened during the night . . . or what he'd dreamed had happened . . . or what he had half dreamed and had half happened . . . whatever . . .

"You woke up in Mars' office?" his father said, startled.

"And there was all this stuff on his computer. Something about a satellite. A weapon, it looked like. Battle Station SS-317—that's what it was called. I don't know what it was, but it looked like top secret stuff."

"Why would a space weapon be in Mars' computer? What's it got to do with MindWar?"

Rick shrugged. "Don't ask me. I'm just telling you what I saw."

"Well, how? How'd you find it? How'd you even get into his machine? The flash drive I gave you is just a security override, not a hack. Mars' keyboard won't even unlock unless it's his fingers that touch it."

"I don't remember what I did," Rick said. "I just woke up and all this stuff was right there on the screen in front of me."

The Traveler nodded thoughtfully as he walked. His spectacles frosted over as the mist from his breath rose up over them. With his watch cap pulled down over his bald head and his scarf pulled up to cover his chin, he looked kind of comical, Rick thought. Just a pair of misted-over glasses in a big overcoat. Like the Invisible Man or something. Even so, Rick could almost feel his dad's powerful mind working through the problem.

"This is definitely worrying," the Traveler said after a moment. "I think your theory that your dreams are giving you a glimpse inside Kurodar's mind is a good one. Baba Yaga . . ."

"That witch woman."

"Yeah—Baba Yaga is the name of a witch from old Russian fairy tales. What you may have been seeing is an image from a story that scared him when he was a child. Those images stick with you even if you don't want them to."

"Right, right," said Rick eagerly. "Like that movie *The Ring* I talked you into letting me watch when I was, like, ten. I still have nightmares about that. Probably Kurodar heard some scary fairy tale when he was a kid and now Baba Yaga lives inside his brain."

"She seems to act as the keeper of his secret thoughts.

The things he remembers but doesn't want to remember . . . Was that what she showed you?"

Rick blew out a long breath that sent the frost swirling up around his face. "I only remember some of it. Really ugly stuff. And it wasn't just images either. It was like I was there." He actually shuddered as he walked. "All around me, there were dead people. So many dead people, Dad . . . and they weren't, like, soldiers from a war or anything either. They were just regular people, like us. Men, and women and children . . . just lying there on the ground like . . . like they'd been tossed away, you know? Like no one even cared about them. And the way their bodies looked. It was like they'd been starved to death. And tortured. And there were living people, too . . . guards. Standing around. Laughing. Laughing at the dead." Rick shook his head, trying to clear the horrors from his mind. "The guards had caps on. Bars on their colors. One had a star on his chest, I remember . . ."

His father's voice came amid a puff of frost over his scarf, under his misted glasses: "Must've been the gulags—the prisons in the Soviet Union. The Communists slaughtered their own people in the tens of millions. Starved them. Tortured them. Enslaved them. And Kurodar's father was one of their key officials. A KGB agent rounding up anyone who might criticize the regime. He must've been particularly brutal. When the Soviet Union fell, Kurodar watched as an angry mob beat his father to death."

"Wow," said Rick. "I get it. So it's, like, maybe Kurodar

keeps these images hidden down inside Baba Yaga's table so he doesn't have to think about what his father was."

"Yes. And what his country was."

"Yeah," said Rick. "I wouldn't want to think about that either."

They were approaching the building that housed the entrance to the underground facilities. The horrifying images were still floating through Rick's mind, as real as reality. He stopped outside the building and his father stopped. Rick turned to the older man—looked at that comical pair of misted glasses between the watch cap and the scarf.

"Why'd they do it?" Rick asked him. His voice was hoarse and soft. "To their own people. Why'd they do it, Dad?"

His father tugged the scarf down onto his chin so he could speak more clearly. His voice was, as it almost always was, calm and clear. "They wanted to make the world a paradise," he said.

Rick was about to answer. He was about to say: "It wasn't paradise. It was hell . . ."

But before he could, the door came open. Miss Ferris was standing there. Her expression—if you could call it an expression—was the same as always: no expression at all.

"It's about time you got here," she said in that flat, toneless voice of hers. "Get inside. This is an emergency."

13. EMERGENCY

"WHAT'S GOING ON?"

As they traveled down in the elevator, Rick's father took off his watch cap and stuffed it into his overcoat pocket. He pulled his scarf down and started to unbutton his coat. His glasses cleared. He looked like himself again: an absentminded egghead. He looked at Miss Ferris, waiting for an answer.

The small, tense, compact woman stared at the door blankly, her lips pressed together to make a thin line. It was odd, thought Rick, stealing a glance at her. Somehow, he had come to like this woman. When he had first become a MindWarrior, he had thought she had no emotions, that she was cold and uncaring. Now, though, he was no longer sure. He thought maybe the truth was: she forced her emotions down so she could do the difficult things she had to do. It wasn't that she didn't care whether or not Rick died in the Realm. It was that she cared so much she couldn't show it, not even to herself.

That was his guess, anyway.

"There was a major breach in our security last night,"

she said. She spoke with as much emotion as the lady in a GPS when she tells you to turn left. "Someone hacked their way into Commander Mars' computer."

Rick and his father exchanged a quick, secret glance. That was Rick! Rick was the emergency! Rick's lips parted. He was about to admit the truth. But his father gave a slight, almost imperceptible shake of his head: *Wait.* They still didn't know whom to trust around here. Rick kept silent.

"No one could have gotten in there without setting off alarms in the compound," Miss Ferris went on. "And no one should have been able to get into the computer itself. That means it must've been Kurodar. If Kurodar's mind has somehow gotten into our compound . . ." She let the sentence trail off, then in the same flat tone, she said: "Well, it would be a disaster."

Again Rick met his father's eyes behind Miss Ferris's back. He didn't want the whole compound to go on red alert because of him. But he could tell by the expression in his father's eyes that he wanted him to keep quiet, so he did.

"So what are we going to do about it?" was all he said.

Miss Ferris gave him a brief, blank glance over her shoulder. "We're sending you back into the Realm to see what you can find out."

The elevator touched down. Miss Ferris strode out and headed down the hall. Rick and his father had to hurry to keep up. She was a small woman, but she took long strides.

"I thought Mars was reluctant to send Rick back in,"

the Traveler said to her back. "I thought he was afraid Rick's mind may have been compromised somehow when he ran through the Breach."

"It's a chance we have to take," she said, marching ahead.

They came into the Portal Room. The techies were already there, four men and two women, each in his or her seat, before his or her screen and keyboard. They all looked like they'd been dragged out of bed to be here. Hair uncombed. One guy with his shirt buttoned wrong. All of them blinking at their machines as if they were dazed.

In the wall at the head of the room was the device Rick always thought of as the glass coffin: the portal into the MindWar Realm. It was a box with a transparent lid, the insides lined with a kind of thin metal. When Rick lay down in the box, the metal wrapped itself around him, and he felt all these pinpricks as the device plugged him into the MindWar system. He hated it. He hated getting in there. It made him claustrophobic. It made him sweat.

Next to the coffin, there was a small set of steps. Next to the steps was Juliet Seven. Juliet Seven was a security guy like Victor One, the only difference being that Victor One was a human being, whereas Rick suspected Juliet Seven might be a cartoon character. He looked like one, anyway. He was so huge and so muscular, he looked as if he were a bunch of gigantic squares and rectangles somehow welded together. Rectangle arms crossed over a square chest under a square head and all of it held up by two legs that looked like cement rectangles. He looked as if he were so strong he could pound you into the ground with a single blow to the top of your head. Which was why Rick never made fun of him for getting stuck with the code name Juliet.

"Let's do this!"

The voice came from behind them, and Rick turned to see Mars enter the room. Rick stopped in his tracks, staring. It had been only a day since he'd last seen Mars, but he'd changed. He'd changed completely.

His solid, angry aspect was gone. He looked disheveled. He looked . . . well, he looked terrified. Instead of his usual crisp dress, he was wearing wrinkled slacks and a wrinkled white shirt, no tie. His silver hair (which Rick sometimes thought was made of steel) was all out of place. And those deep-set glaring eyes of his were staring out at them like the eyes of a hunted animal hiding in a dark cave.

Up until that moment, Rick had not imagined Mars could even feel an emotion like fear. But Rick could see it was worse than that. Mars wasn't just afraid. He was in a complete panic. Totally messed up.

Why? Rick wondered. *What's he so scared about? Is it because I got into his computer?*

And his father's questions came back to him: *Why would a space weapon be in Mars' computer. What's that got to do with MindWar?*

Something was wrong here, Rick sensed. Something was terribly wrong. Maybe he shouldn't get in the coffin.

Maybe he shouldn't do what Mars and Miss Ferris wanted him to do.

"We're sending you back to your last location," said Miss Ferris. She pressed a button and the lid of the glass coffin opened.

Rick turned to look at the opening box. Maybe . . .

"We need to find out what's happening," Mars said. "We need to find out how Kurodar is getting into our systems. Sending security bots through cyberspace into reality. Hacking our computers . . ."

Mars's words tumbled together as he spoke. He was so panicked he couldn't even speak right.

Miss Ferris was gesturing at him to climb the stairs, to get into the box, the portal into the Realm. Rick hesitated another moment. He wasn't sure what to do.

He glanced at his father. The Traveler took a breath. "Maybe we need to think about this," he said quietly.

Mars took a threatening step toward him. "You don't have a say in this, Dial. Your country's safety is at stake. More than that: the world's safety. We have no time to stand here and talk about it."

The commander and the Traveler locked eyes, Mars's furious glare meeting Dial's steady gaze.

Then, after a moment, Rick's father turned to him. "It's your decision," he said.

Mars looked at him too. So did Miss Ferris.

Rick nodded. "Yeah," he said. "I'll go."

Mars was right. The Boar Soldier in the tower. The

hack of Mars's computer. Something was going on. And if he could enter the Realm and find out what Kurodar was up to . . .

"Let's do it," he said.

He climbed up the steps into the portal box and lay down without saying another word.

Immediately, Miss Ferris pressed the button that closed the box's lid. Even before the metal lining began to wrap around him, Rick started to sweat with claustrophobic panic. He felt the pinpricks as his nervous system was plugged into the computers. Soon, the familiar floating feeling came over him. Darkness surrounded him. A portal of light formed above him.

Here we go, he thought.

He focused his mind on the portal of light and . . .

Like water slipping through a straw, he was through.

He was through—and, the very next instant, he was being hurled into infinite blackness, heading for death so quickly there was no time to stop it, no time at all.

14. DEAD SPACE

TERROR GRIPPED HIS heart. Wild, unreasoning terror flashing through every nerve ending. He fell and fell through nothing, total nothing, with nothing to stop him, nothing to reach for or hold on to, nothing to keep him from hurtling forever through this nightmare of absolute emptiness.

He understood at once what was happening. It was the darkness inside the sarcophagus. It was the darkness that Favian had told him about.

The darkness spread over everything everywhere. The Scarlet Plain. The Blue Wood. The Golden City is all that's left of MindWar.

It was true. The church sarcophagus had afforded a glimpse of all that was left of the MindWar Realm. Beyond the Golden City and its dead, there was nothing but this. This utter nothingness. And he was falling into the heart of it.

As he fell, even as he fell, he felt as if he were being crushed and suffocated by the unending night. Somehow, the blackness was a living thing, closing on him, devouring him with malice, with relish.

Rick understood this too. The darkness was not just darkness. It came out of Kurodar's mind. It was the very hell of the terrorist's heart, the evil at the center of it.

And it was eating him alive!

Down and down and down he went. The agony, the terror, the whirling rush to death—there was no stopping it!

Never in his life had Rick felt so helpless, so hopeless, and so afraid. The rush, the blackness, the living evil. Falling into nothing, nothing, nothing!

His mind began to fade. His thinking grew dim and distant. His very consciousness was fading. Life itself . . .

He knew what would happen if he died in the Realm. The long, horrifying living decay . . . He'd seen it. Desperate, he tried to come up with a way to stop himself. But . . .

There's nothing . . . , he thought in a panic. *It's all blackness. There's nothing anywhere to use or grab or cling to . . . There's nothing here at all!*

But no, wait. Wait, that wasn't right, was it? There *was* something, he realized. There was him. There was still him. He was still thinking, right? So he was still here. And Mariel had taught him that by focusing the power of his spirit, he could change the very substance of the Realm.

He tried it. He tried to focus his spirit on the blackness . . .

But he could tell at once: it was no good. The blackness

was too deep, too complete, too all-encompassing. It *had* no substance. There was nothing he could focus on, nothing he could change, and even if there were, his spirit was not large enough, strong enough to affect that seemingly infinite abyss . . .

It was hopeless. He fell and fell and the devouring night was endless. Nothing but blackness. Blackness and his own fading spirit . . .

But then . . . another thought . . . another idea . . . If he was here . . . If he was still here . . .

In the midst of that dying rush of terror, he heard his mother's voice.

You'll never go anywhere alone. I promise.

If he was still here . . . and if he was not alone . . . if he was never alone . . .

The logic of it clicked into place and suddenly, almost magically, Rick was himself again. His despair vanished— even his terror dulled—and he was all action: the quarterback, Number 12, the guy who never cracked or gave up under pressure. Never. Not even now. Not even here.

The living blackness was too powerful for him to change. So he focused his spirit beyond the blackness . . . beyond nothing . . . beyond even his own death . . .

And at once, he could feel it. His mother was right. He was not alone.

Rick steadied himself. He focused beyond the darkness of Kurodar's heart, beyond the darkness of his own destruction. Without his even thinking about it, the focus of his spirit changed. The focus turned into prayer. But it was no ordinary prayer. There were no words in it. It was instead a prayer he made with his whole self, the deepest self of himself. His very spirit reached across the seemingly endless blackness to the place where the blackness ended, where the endlessness itself ended, to the Spirit from which his own spirit had its source. He could not see this Spirit—he could not even sense the hundreth part of its eternal vastness—but he recognized it. He knew it all the same. His father had been teaching him about it since he was a little boy . . .

So he prayed—prayed in that wordless way with his entire being.

And the darkness tore. It ripped apart like paper.

Light.

A portal.

Rick did not say thank you. He did not have to. His whole spirit had turned to gratitude.

He went into the light.

15. BETRAYAL

RICK AWOKE IN the glass coffin and started screaming. The coffin lid was shut, its surface inches from his face. The metal foil was still wrapped tightly around him, holding him close like a cocoon. He could still feel the million tiny pinpricks going into his flesh.

The claustrophobia was overwhelming. He needed to get out of here. Like, now.

He yelled and struggled, his powerful arms pushing against the metal, bending it out of shape.

"Get me out of here! Get me out!" he shouted.

He felt as if at any moment the blackness would surround him again. He was terrified he might be sucked back into the Realm, sent hurtling, whirling, back into that animate nothingness.

"Help! Get me out!"

Over his own screams, he heard a sort of *chuck* sound and then a hiss. The glass lid of the coffin started rising. Rick continued to thrash and push against the metal that held him.

The next moment, Miss Ferris was there, bending

over him. She spoke in that same monotone as always, but even in his panic, Rick could see the warmth of concern in her eyes.

"Hold still. Hold still, Rick," she said. "You'll hurt yourself. You'll be out in a second."

Panting with panic, Rick forced himself to hold still. Sure enough, the metal wrapping began to open. He could barely wait for it to free him. As soon as he was able, he pushed out, reaching for the edges of the coffin to pull himself free. Miss Ferris tried to help him, but he was too big for her. She stepped aside. The next moment, Juliet Seven was there. The massive cartoon character of a man clamped a square hand around Rick's arm and practically hoisted him out of the box.

Rick nearly fell down the stairs to the Portal Room floor. He dropped to his knees. The room seemed to spin around him. He gagged. He felt like he was going to throw up.

That blackness . . . that awful living evil blackness . . . He had been sure it was going to devour him. He didn't know why it hadn't. There'd been nothing to stop his fall. Nothing to hold on to. In the fog of the present moment, in the daze of his return, in his sickness, he could not remember how in the world he'd gotten out of there.

Now he was aware that his father was at his side, kneeling next to him, a hand on his shoulder.

"What happened?" the Traveler said. "What did you see?"

Rick gagged again. "It was awful," he said, still panting.

"It was worse than awful. It was, like, the worst thing that ever happened . . ."

But before he could finish, things got even worse.

As Rick remained on his knees, sick and panting—as his father kneeled beside him, holding his arm, blinking with concern behind his round glasses—the door to the Portal Room hissed open and two security guards charged in. They were big men with big rifles strapped over their shoulders. They looked ready for unpleasant business.

In confusion, Rick looked up and saw Commander Mars stepping toward the soldiers. Rick could tell that Mars had been expecting them, that he'd known they were coming. The thought flashed through his mind: *He must've called them.*

It was true. Frowning grimly, Mars pointed down at where Rick's father knelt beside him.

He said, "Put this man under arrest."

Before anyone could react, the two guards grabbed Lawrence Dial under his arms and hauled him to his feet.

"What?" said Rick. He could still just barely think. "What are you doing?"

But his father remained calm even now. Held captive by the soldiers, he merely turned to Mars with a quiet look and a slight smile.

"Even you must know this is a mistake, Mars," he said.

Mars took another step. He leaned in close to the Traveler's face and peered into his glasses, his expression triumphant.

"You're under arrest for treason, Dial," Mars said. "I'll see to it you go to prison for life. In fact, you're lucky I don't just have you shot." Then to the guards he said, "Get him out of here. Jail him in the hospital secure room."

The guards began to drag the Traveler to the door. Rage swept over Rick. Weak as he was, he leapt to his feet. He began to charge at Commander Mars. He had some crazy idea of tackling him, driving him into the floor. Not that that would have changed anything, but Rick could be a hotheaded guy at times and this was definitely one of those times.

He meant to charge at Mars, but he never took a single step. Before he could move, Juliet Seven grabbed his arms from behind, locked his elbows in a grip like steel. Rick struggled against him, but even a big man like Number 12 was no match for Juliet Seven.

Mars sneered at him. "If you're not careful, you'll be next."

Rick watched helplessly as the soldiers marched Lawrence Dial out of the room. Mars followed after them. And the Portal Room door hissed shut behind them all.

THE DEAD
ATTACK

16. MINDJACK

KURODAR HOWLED IN pain. The cry was so loud even his workers heard it outside. The workers paused with their shovels in the air and raised their heads to listen. The howl went on a long time, like the cry of a wolf greeting the moon. Then it faded away. The sounds of the surrounding jungle closed in again. After a moment or two, the workers went back to what they had been doing: tossing the last dirt over the grave of the assassin—Harold Hepplewhite—whom their master had destroyed as if by some kind of bizarre and terrifying magic.

None of the workers in Kurodar's jungle outpost knew exactly how it had happened. The hitman Hepplewhite had been their last hope of getting free of this place. They had prayed he would kill Kurodar so they could leave. But somehow Kurodar seemed to have eliminated the assassin with nothing more than a thought. That was the end of all their hopes. The workers knew they would be too afraid to try to escape now. Such power as Kurodar's could reach them anywhere, kill them anywhere, them and their families. They had begun to believe Kurodar was some sort of demon. They had begun to feel they were trapped in a kind of hell.

But Kurodar was not a demon. Nor was he, as he had sometimes thought himself, any kind of a god. He was just a man—a brilliant man, but still just a man—a sick man attached to a machine that gave him power. And right this moment, that machine was causing him unbelievable agony.

It happened when the boy Dial had reentered the Realm. Kurodar had been hoping this would happen. He had been waiting for it like a spider waiting on his web. The moment the Traveler's son attempted to return to the blackness of his inner space, he was planning to devour him, to take the young Dial's mind into himself and digest everything the boy knew and everything he was. He would have stolen his secrets and transformed the big, handsome hero into a shriveled shell, interminably decaying into death. The very thought delighted him.

He had almost succeeded at it too. Everything was going exactly as he'd wanted. He had the boy in the heart of his darkness and was on the verge of obliterating him, making him part of that dark and then . . . and then—somehow—suddenly—

Suddenly, a pain like nothing he had ever felt before went through Kurodar's very core. Something deep in his spirit—something deep and essential—tore open. That's what it felt like. Like his soul was a piece of canvas and someone had ripped a hole right through the center of it. Strapped to his machines in the cellar of his jungle outpost,

Kurodar howled and howled—sending up that noise that had made the gravediggers stop their work to listen.

And when he stopped howling, the boy—this Rick Dial, who had plagued him past tolerance—was gone.

Well, maybe not gone. No, not gone entirely. The connection between Kurodar and the Dial boy was still in place. Kurodar could still get to him, get through him, get what he needed. But it wasn't going to be as simple as devouring him whole. It was going to take a tremendous effort. And it was going to take time.

Ever since Rick had gone through Kurodar's Breach, Kurodar's mind and Kurodar's circuits and the circuits of Rick's mind had all become interconnected. Ever since that one moment when Rick passed through the border between the Realm and RL, Kurodar had had a presence in Rick's consciousness. It had been a small presence at first—very small—but Kurodar had understood at once that it might be just what he needed to get behind the enemy's defenses. He had immediately gone to work making his small presence larger.

In order to do this, Kurodar had begun to concentrate his energies. Rick had destroyed his fortress. He had brought down his WarCraft. The Axis Assembly had withdrawn its funding. Kurodar needed to focus all his power for one final attack. It was with great sorrow he let the beautiful Realm he had painstakingly created fall back into the shadow of nothingness, but it had to be done. Instead, he had condensed all the power of his mind and his machinery on the Golden City, his interface with cyberspace. From the Golden City, he was now able to unleash a massive effort of will. With that effort, he was able to build a new outpost, not in a computer this time but in Rick Dial's brain.

The results had been wonderful, almost miraculous. Whenever Rick slept, whenever his consciousness relaxed, Kurodar could enter his mind and work on building his presence. His outpost in Rick had grown so strong, he had actually been able to send one of his security bots through it—straight out of the Realm and through Rick's consciousness and directly into RL to kill one of the compound's guards. That had been a neat trick—but neater still, Kurodar had been able to control Rick himself. While Rick slept, Kurodar had used Rick's own knowledge to send the boy into the MindWar compound's underground complex. He used Rick's own mind to project himself into Mars's computer, hacking through its security. And there he had found exactly what he suspected he would. Exactly what he needed.

The Battle Station! His rivals in the Axis Assembly had thought they could hide this from him, but of course they could hide nothing. Commander Mars had been using the Traveler's MindWar defense technology to hack the most secure U.S. government systems and smuggle out specs and codes to the greatest American weapons system ever devised. Now Kurodar had used Rick Dial to access those specs and codes. If he could just finish reading the designs out of Rick's consciousness, he would be in possession of a weapon with destructive power beyond imagining. The Axis thought they could get hold of this machine through the usual clunky human means: treachery and greed. But Kurodar would show them that the Realm machinery was a far better tool than mere unreliable humanity.

The Battle Station, he now knew, was a top secret weapon launched into space by the United States about a year and a half ago. It had been sent up disguised as a weather satellite, but it was not that, nothing like it. It was in fact a hugely powerful device that could soak up the energy of the sun, concentrate it in a single blast, and direct that blast at the earth for a sustained period. Used properly, the device could draw a massive swath of fire and death across an entire continent. With the Battle Station under his control, Kurodar would be able to literally set the United States ablaze.

If Kurodar could just digest the inside of Rick Dial's mind, he would have the codes and signals he needed to take control of the Battle Station and set it into motion. But he had to act fast. He had to act before the Axis got hold of the codes themselves through their own transaction with the MindWar compound.

He needed a delaying tactic. He needed to use Rick Dial's mind as a portal again, to attack the MindWar compound and keep them busy while he took control of the Battle Station.

There was only one problem. The link between Rick's

mind and Kurodar's went both ways. As Kurodar had been working on Rick's mind, Rick had been entering the Realm, albeit unconsciously, in his sleep. Kurodar could not let the Realm go undefended or Dial might go in there and destroy it. Given that Kurodar and the Realm were now utterly linked together, the destruction of the Realm would almost surely mean the destruction of Kurodar himself.

So before he attacked the MindWar compound, Kurodar had to create a new defender for the Realm, someone who could stop Rick Dial if he dared to attack him, someone more powerful than the demon Reza and even greater than the Octo-Guardian.

He knew just how to do it. Those other monsters—those had been creatures created out of the minds of other humans. But this monster, this greatest of all monsters, would come directly out of his own mind. This would be a product of his own darkest imagination.

Kurodar knew where to find the template of the beast. He would make him in the image of his own father.

Kurodar had loved his father. He had idolized him. Worshipped him as if he were a god. But he had also feared him. And with good reason. His father had been brutally cruel to him when he was a boy. He had beat him black-and-blue for the slightest disobedience. He had continually mocked him for his ugliness and his weakness. He had locked him away inside a closet, some-times for days, to "teach him strength and discipline and manliness." Kurodar knew why all the people were afraid of the KGB colonel. Wherever he went, terror and pain followed after.

Kurodar had not blamed his father for this. Not at all. He knew his father was a great man and that he himself was, in fact, an ugly little child, unhealthy and intellectual, a great disappointment to his powerhouse of a dad. No, Kurodar had felt his father was right to abuse him. He felt he deserved to be ridiculed, deserved to be beaten, deserved to be locked away. After all, his father was like a god to him. He wouldn't do anything wrong, would he?

Now, as the dreadful agony of Rick Dial's escape from the Realm began to subside, as the hole that had been torn in his spirit began to mend, as his mind began to clear, he turned his power of imagination back to the work of creation. He saw his father now. He pictured him in his mind's eye. He imagined the KGB man as he had been before he died . . .

Yes! he thought.

He would bring him back to life now. He would re-create his father in cyber form and place him as a guardian over the last bastion of the Realm. He would resurrect him as the giant he was, the demigod he was. He would set him up as the master of the armies of the Golden City, the leader of its defenses. If Rick Dial, or anyone else, tried to invade Kurodar's domain, they would find themselves doing battle against the most terrifying security bot anyone could imagine . . .

Kurodar focused and worked the circuits. Deep in the heart of the Realm, in the center of the Golden City, a figure began to emerge into being.

A beast from his worst nightmares.

His father made monstrous.

The King of the Dead.

17. SPY HUNTER

MOLLY SMILED TO herself as she finished packing. She worked carefully to fold a last sweater and lay it neatly in the small suitcase lying open on her bed, but her mind was far away. She was still thinking about last night, about Rick, about kissing Rick under the moonlit trees.

There's only you.

These last few weeks—what a wild journey it had been. A crazy way to find the man of your dreams, that was for sure. Especially when it turned out the MOYD was one of your oldest friends. Other girls went to parties. Other girls went on dates. Other girls met their guys in all kinds of places. Molly? She'd been kidnapped, manhandled, chased by gunmen, nearly killed. She'd done hand-to-hand combat against thugs twice her size and killers with automatic weapons and flying drones that dealt death from the sky. She'd helped foil a plot to destroy the capital. And she'd been rescued from death by a guy driving a spaceship that seemed to have zipped right out of a video game and into real life. And all of it had finally brought her and Rick together.

Not the usual *How I Met Your Father* scenario. She doubted her children would believe her when she told them!

Now—in a few minutes—the transport truck would be here to take her and her dad away. By order of Commander Mars, she was heading home. Back to Putnam Hills, back to her college life, back to the same old same old.

But the truth was the same old same old would never be the same.

Before she was kidnapped, her mind had been mired in confusion. She knew she had feelings for Rick, but he seemed to have abandoned her. She was constantly thinking about it, torturing herself with questions. Did she feel this way or that way? Should she do this or that?

She remembered that kiss under the trees again. Smiled to herself again. All those questions were answered now.

She patted the sweater into place and zipped the case shut. She took hold of the handle and drew the suitcase off the bed, set it on the floor. She turned to take a last survey of the bare barracks room in which she'd been staying, panning her eyes over the place to make sure she wasn't leaving anything behind.

She turned—and then she stopped turning and gasped at the sight of the gray corpse-like face staring in at her through the window with bloodshot eyes.

"Victor!" she whispered.

Victor One was pressed up against the glass, holding to the windowsill to keep himself on his feet. He really did look like a corpse. His cheeks were the color of stone. His

136

eyes were streaked with branching red lines of blood. His mouth was open. His stare was empty. Molly was sure he was going to fall over any minute.

She rushed to the window. Unlocked it. Hoisted it open.

"Molly . . . ," Victor One whispered weakly. His body bent forward, his head coming into the room.

Frightened, confused, Molly glanced up quickly at the scene behind him: a sere treeless stretch of the compound that ran to a section of barbed wire. She understood: Victor must've snuck here from the hospital, using back ways to avoid being seen by the guards.

She put a hand on his arm. "What are you doing out of bed? You've got to get back to the hospital. What's the matter? What's wrong?"

Without a word, the bodyguard began to try to climb in over the sill through the window. But even though the window was low to the ground, he didn't have the strength to drag himself through it.

Molly grabbed hold of him, one arm around his shoulders, trying to steady him. "Victor. Stop. Wait. You'll hurt yourself. What're you doing?"

"Help me," was all he said to her. His voice was barely a whisper.

"I'm not strong enough to lift you through," she said. "Let me walk you around front. I'll let you in the door."

V-One shook his head, still trying to claw himself up over the windowsill. "Guards out front. Coming this way.

Once they realize I left the hospital . . . they'll be all over . . . Please . . ."

"All right, all right," she said. She didn't know what else to do. "Steady. I'll help you."

Getting the best grip on the big man she could, she began to try to lift him up over the sill. She couldn't do much, but it was just the extra help he needed. He got his leg up on the edge of the window and practically spilled through as Molly tried to catch him. She was strong, but he was too heavy. She staggered back as he tumbled into her. She lost her hold on him and Victor One dropped to the floor with a thud. He curled up on his side and lay at her feet, breathing hard.

"Victor . . . ," she said, but before she could speak another word, there was a knock at the door.

"You all right, Molly?" It was her father, Professor Jameson. "I thought I heard something fall in there. Are you okay?"

"I'm fine, Daddy," she called back. "I just dropped . . . something."

"The truck should be here any minute."

"I'm almost ready," she said. "I'll be . . . I'll be right out."

"Okay."

She heard her father's footsteps trailing away down the hall.

Victor One, meanwhile, had caught his breath, gathered his strength. He was working his way up into a sitting position. Leaning back against the wall beside the window. Wearily pushing the brown hair off his gray face. Drawing a deep breath to steady himself.

Molly knelt down in front of him on one knee. She touched his shoulder gently, spoke softly. "What are you doing here, V-One? Why'd you leave the hospital?"

He looked at her and the sight of his bloodshot eyes filled her with pity and fear. He did not look like he would live another hour.

"Mars . . . ," he said, flinching with pain at the effort of speaking. "He arrested the Traveler . . ."

"What? Professor Dial? Arrested him? Why?"

Victor had to take another breath before he could talk again and when he did talk, his voice was low and rasping. "Last night . . . someone overrode the compound's security system . . . hacked Mars' computer . . . Mars claims he has evidence linking the security override to a program written by the Traveler. And he says only Kurodar could have hacked the computer. So he's saying the Traveler . . ."

Victor One ran out of strength and had to take a breath, but Molly finished the sentence for him. "He's saying the Traveler is a traitor working with Kurodar."

Victor One nodded weakly.

"That's impossible," Molly said.

Victor One nodded again. "I know. And Mars knows too."

"Mars knows . . . ? But if he knows, then why . . . ?"

"Because Mars . . . Mars is the one. Mars is the traitor."

Molly stared at him, her mind blank, stunned into silence.

Victor One continued to work the words out slowly, fighting the pain. "He's afraid the Traveler found out what he was doing when he got into his computer . . . He's accusing him first, to ruin his reputation, so no one will believe him when he tells the truth."

"That . . . Wait, what? How do you know this?"

"Moros . . . ," was all Victor One could manage to say.

"Moros . . . ?" Then Molly remembered. "The billionaire who owned the swampland where they held me when I was kidnapped."

"I put my Army Intelligence guys onto him. Moros has been playing a double game, helping to fund Kurodar but at the same time trying to broker a deal between Mars and the Axis . . . Mars used the MindWar program as a giant hack into U.S. defense systems. Stole plans . . . weapons . . . codes . . . to sell to Moros . . . who'll auction them off to the highest bidder . . ."

"But why? Why would he do that?"

Victor One gave a brief, coughing, cynical laugh. "A billion dollars."

"A billion . . . But I thought Mars was such a big patriot . . ."

Victor One's head fell back weakly against the wall. He looked up at the ceiling. He closed his eyes.

"Mars stinks," he said.

Molly's confusion was passing now. Her mind was coming back online. She was trying to understand the situation, trying to figure out what they had to do next. Mars, the head of the MindWar Project, was an agent of the Axis Assembly . . . Professor Dial was under arrest, charged with treason . . . And what about . . . ?

"Rick," she whispered. "Is Rick all right?"

Victor One opened his eyes. He smiled at her, but the color seemed to have drained out of his blue eyes. It was as if he were looking at her from another place far away.

"Your lover boy's all right," he said, trying to make a joke of it. "For now, anyway. They tried to send him into the Realm again and something happened. I'm not sure what. He came back shaken up, but he's all right. They're doing tests on him at the hospital barracks now. But I heard him in there, yelling that he wanted to see his dad. Sounded like his usual hothead self."

Molly tried to smile at that, but her emotions overpowered her. "We have to help him," she said softly. "We have to stop Mars . . . Can we get word out to your military friends?"

"Mars has got the compound on lockdown," Victor One half whispered. "For 'security reasons,' he says. No one comes or goes without his specific approval. He's jamming cell phones, stopping all communications out of here. I can't even get online anymore. My guess is he wants to make his trade with Moros and then make a run for it with his billion."

"But I'm leaving. My dad and I. In a few minutes. Maybe when I get out, I can contact Army Intelligence..."

Victor One shook his head. "I'm working off the grid. By the time you reached my contacts, this'll all be over. And the stuff I know you can't know, Molly. It has to be me who goes..."

"But look at you, you can barely move."

"It has to be me."

"But if I can bring them here..."

"Mars'll be long gone. I'm telling you. You've got to figure out a way to get me out of here."

"Get...?" Molly lifted her eyes to the ceiling. It was so much, so fast. She said a quick prayer and felt her mind steady. She lowered her eyes to Victor again.

Boy, he looked bad! Really bad. Like he might just fall over and die any minute. How was she going to get him out of the compound when he could hardly walk... and when Mars had guards everywhere...

V-One seemed to read her mind. "Don't worry about me," he said. "I may look like I'm dying... I may *be* dying... But that won't stop me."

Molly rolled her eyes. Guys like Victor One—and guys like Rick Dial for that matter—they all thought they were supermen. Swaggering, stubborn, unstoppable when they set their minds to something. They all thought they were magically indestructible.

It was kind of what she liked about them.

"All right," she said quietly. "We'll get you out. Somehow."

There was a knock at the door. Her father called in: "The truck's here, Molly."

Molly nodded. Took a breath. She leaned close to Victor One and spoke into his ear.

"Here's what we're going to do," she said.

18. THE GATE

MOLLY STOOD IN the cold outside her barracks. She could feel her heart fluttering in her chest like a caged bird. The transport truck that was to take them back to Putnam Hills had come in through the compound's front gate. It was parked just beyond the guard checkpoint there, waiting for them to bring their suitcases over.

Molly watched as her father walked toward the checkpoint. He was trying to look casual, but she could tell he was nervous. The driver of the truck—a small, sloppy soldier with his shirt nearly untucked from his pants—was leaning against the side of the truck. Professor Jameson approached him and spoke to him. The driver shook his head: no.

"Come on," whispered Molly. It wasn't just the cold that made her shiver.

Her father spoke a few more words, making small encouraging gestures with his hands.

He has to bring the truck over here, thought Molly. *He has to.*

Every second that went by, her plan became more

dangerous. Mars might change his mind and decide she and her father couldn't leave. Or someone might notice V-One had left the hospital and sound the alarm. Or one of the guards might just decide to wander by here . . .

They were everywhere, those guards. Watching from the towers, marching along the barbed-wire fence that sealed the compound's perimeter. Moving from barracks to barracks. It was funny, Molly thought. When she had come to this place a week or so ago, Molly had thought of the MindWar compound as a friendly outpost. She had been through a terrible ordeal. Kidnapped. Imprisoned. Chased through the woods. Very nearly killed. She needed rest; medical attention. She was glad to get inside the fence. All those guards—they were there to protect her. The whole place was operated by the American government after all. It was safe here. She was safe.

Now, suddenly, the place had turned into a prison. All because of Mars. All because Mars had sold out his country.

Molly saw the truck driver make a gesture of surrender, throwing up his hands. She let out a breath as he turned to get back into the truck. In another moment, he was starting up the engine. Her father was walking back toward her.

"Okay," Professor Jameson said. "He's bringing it right up to the door, like you asked." Father's and daughter's eyes locked for a moment and an understanding passed between them. Molly had told her dad what she was planning to do.

The truck was a typical Army transport vehicle: a railed flatbed with a domed canvas covering. It rocked and rumbled over the half-frozen ground as it moved away from the front gate and swung around toward their small barracks house. As it pulled up in front of Molly, the driver looked out at her. He had a round, brown-skinned face with a sorrowful expression, as if the world were continually hurting his feelings. He seemed deeply burdened by the fact that he'd had to drive over to the barracks to pick Molly up.

Molly answered his frown with the brightest, prettiest smile she could muster.

"Thanks so much for coming!" she said up at the window. "That is so sweet of you."

The driver shrugged.

"I was wondering if you could help me with my bag?" she went on. "It's a little heavy for me."

Which was ridiculous. Molly was an athlete and could easily have hurled the bag to the front gate from where she was standing. But she knew that guys like to help girls lift stuff—it is an iron law of life—and though she didn't like to fool people, the situation was desperate and the cause was just.

The driver sighed, but, sorrowful or not, he was a guy and he liked to help girls lift stuff and he didn't hesitate. He got down out of the cab of the truck and followed Molly into the barracks. She led him down the hall to her room and pointed to the suitcase. When he saw it, he paused. Then he turned and gave her a look. Well, it was pretty ridiculous, all right. The suitcase was so small and Molly was such a big, strong girl.

But she smiled again and looked up at the ceiling. "I have a bad back," she said. "And I don't like to ask my dad." She didn't even sound convincing to herself.

The truck driver nodded sadly. This whole business was a pain in the neck to him, but he did like Molly's smile. So he made a face—*Whatever*—and he picked up the suitcase and carried it back down the hall.

The truck stood waiting outside and so did Professor Jameson. To Molly's eyes, her dad looked as nervous as a cat stuck in a dryer. She could only hope the driver wouldn't notice.

Molly held her breath as the driver pulled open the truck's rear gate. Inside, under the canvas, there were several stacked wooden crates—and Victor One.

With her father's help, V-One had come around the side of the house and climbed into the truck while Molly and the driver were inside. Molly could see him in there, way at the back of the truck's interior. He was hidden behind a crate, and the covering canvas draped him in shadow, but his eyes gleamed clearly. Molly was sure the driver would spot him.

But the driver just wanted to get out of there and was barely paying any attention at all. He tossed her suitcase in, closed the gate, and tromped back to the driver's side of the cab without a word. Without a word, he climbed up behind the wheel. When Molly and Professor Jameson hesitated—stunned they had actually managed to smuggle Victor One on board—the driver finally leaned out and barked impatiently, "Let's go, all right?"

Molly and Professor Jameson came to life and climbed quickly into the cab. It was close with all three of them in there. Molly was wedged in tightly between the driver behind the wheel and her dad by the window.

The driver started the truck and the vehicle began rumbling toward the gate of the compound.

No one spoke. Molly bit her lip nervously. She stared through the windshield as the gate came closer. Two guards stepped out of their guardhouse to greet them and check their pass to make sure they had Mars's permission to leave. Molly was now so tense she felt as if she had slipped into some faraway place inside her own mind. The scene outside seemed almost unreal to her, as if the truck windshield were a movie screen and the sentries waiting out there with their rifles on their shoulders were just images being projected onto it.

The driver began to slow the truck. He lowered the window. He fished his travel pass out of his pocket. He stopped the truck. He held the pass up for the sentry to see. The sentry took the pass and examined it. He glanced inside the cab to make sure only Molly and Professor Jameson were in there. He nodded to the second sentry. The second sentry pulled a small lever in a gray box and the compound gate slowly began to swing open.

Molly took a deep breath of relief. They were going to make it. They were going to pull this off. Soon they'd be outside the compound and Victor One could alert Army Intelligence. The Army would send soldiers to arrest Mars, to free Professor Dial, to save Rick . . .

Outside the truck, a phone rang in the sentry's pocket.

Molly's eyes flashed to him. The sentry was a young man with a very pale face and very innocent-looking eyes. He pulled the phone out of his pocket and spoke into it in a low voice. The front gate, meanwhile, was continuing its slow swing open. The young sentry listened to the phone for a moment.

"Yes, sir," he said then.

He put the phone back in his pocket. He held a finger out to the second sentry. The second sentry touched the gate lever. The lever stopped swinging. It was about half-way open now.

Molly's heart turned dark. She felt it sinking inside her.

The young sentry turned back to the driver and crooked his finger at him.

"Would you step out of the truck for a minute, please?" he said.

The driver's eyes rolled heavenward in his sorrowful face. "Sure," he said sarcastically. "It's not like I'm in a hurry or anything."

"Sorry," said the young sentry. "Orders. We have to take a look in the back of the truck. We're on lockdown. Security. You know."

"Sure, sure," the sad-faced driver said wearily. He put the truck in park. The engine rumbled in idle.

Molly could barely breathe at all. She felt her stomach turn to acid. She looked longingly through the windshield at the gate. The gate stood tantalizingly ajar. Just wide enough to get the truck through . . . maybe . . . at the right angle . . .

But there was no chance of that now. The driver was opening the cab door. The young sentry was already moving toward the back of the truck. It would take only a second: they'd open the truck gate and look inside and spot Victor One and it would be over. Mars would have them completely trapped inside the compound.

Molly glanced at her father. Professor Jameson watched helplessly as the guard began to climb down out of the cab.

Frantically, Molly's eyes moved . . . to the dashboard . . . to the steering wheel . . . to the side mirror where she saw the young sentry waiting beside the rear of the truck . . .

The truck's motor was still grumbling in idle . . .

The driver stepped out of the cab. When she heard his feet hit the frozen ground, Molly slid quickly over the seat and got behind the wheel. She reached out of the cab and seized hold of the door handle. She pulled the door shut.

Startled, the driver swung around at the noise. "Hey!" he said.

Molly put the truck in reverse. Quickly, she checked the side mirror. She could see the young sentry still standing beside the truck, not directly behind it. She wouldn't hit him if she backed up.

That was all she needed to know. She drove her sneaker down hard on the gas.

Molly had to back up if she was going to get the right angle on the half-open gate, if she was to have any chance at all of driving the truck through it, out of the compound. The truck roared and went rattling backward. It shot past the young sentry. He just stood there, gaping at it as it went by.

That was far enough. Molly hit the brake. The truck jolted to a stop. She grabbed the gear shift.

Professor Jameson looked at her in horror. He was only just now beginning to realize what his daughter was planning to do.

"Molly!" he shouted.

"We've got to!" Molly shouted back.

"Stop!" the young guard shouted outside.

But Molly didn't stop. She threw the truck into gear. She stomped on the gas again. The truck shot forward. Molly saw the half-open gate speeding at the windshield.

The gate came closer and closer, fast. The way out was narrow. The gate's edge looked like it was going to clip the fender, stop the truck.

Molly wrenched the wheel. The truck bounced right. There was just enough room to squeeze through the gate if she hit it just so. At least she hoped there was. It wasn't going to be easy at this speed, and her speed was increasing every second.

The gate came rushing at her. Closer.

And then the second sentry stepped in the way.

He held up his hand. "Stop!" he shouted boldly.

Molly kept her foot jammed down on the gas pedal. The truck rumbled over the frozen earth toward the sentry. He had to move.

"Molly!" her father shouted again. "You'll kill him!"

He was right. Molly watched as the sentry grew larger in the windshield. Another second, she'd run him over. She had to stop.

But the sentry broke first. As the truck raced toward him, the bold expression on his face melted into a wide-eyed look of surprise and fear. Suddenly, he was moving, rushing to the side, racing to get out of the way.

The gate was clear. Molly gave the truck full gas. It charged like a wild bull at the opening.

But she didn't clear it.

The next moment—a jolt—a teeth-rattling squeak— the metal of the gate scratched the side of the truck—a jarring crash—the edge of the gate hit the side mirror and ripped it right off.

Molly let out a cry. But she kept her foot down.

And the truck bounced forward and flew through the gate at high speed.

They were out. They were out! Molly saw the forest

and the forest road spreading before her. She felt her heart expand as a blast of joy went through her. She laughed out loud.

"We're going to make it!" she shouted to her dad over the engine noise.

And then the creatures attacked.

19. INVASION

MOLLY HAD NO time to react. She couldn't react. She couldn't even believe what she was seeing. Out of nowhere, out of nothing, a hideous creature materialized in the air. It was a gray, winged, woman-like thing, its shrieking face half flesh, half skull. It swept down on the truck with its spindly arms outstretched, its hands outreaching, its long talons slicing, and its teeth bared.

Molly screamed.

The Harpy smashed into the windshield full force. The truck stuttered. A web of cracks shot out across the glass. The beast's hideous face was pressed against the cracks, inches from Molly.

Molly convulsively wrenched the wheel. The truck careened leftward, out of control. It sped off the road. It bounced over the ground. And then, still traveling fast, it smashed into a tree.

Metal crunched. Glass broke. The truck's engine died. Molly's body was thrown forward. Her forehead smacked the steering wheel—not hard, but hard enough to hurt. The Harpy, meanwhile, lost its grip in the crash and was hurled off the windshield, still shrieking.

Molly sat straight, dazed, and saw the winged creature pinwheel away to her left. It landed hard on the forest
floor. A fizzle of purple static lanced through its form
like bolts of lightning. Then, the next second, the Harpy
flashed and vanished and was gone.

Molly blinked. Her head aching, her mind clouded.

Did that just happen?

She turned dully to her father.

"Dad? Are you all right?"

The professor in the passenger seat raised a hand to
reassure her, but his lip was bleeding. He was breathing
hard. He couldn't speak at first.

"What . . . ?" said Molly, swallowing. "Did you see
that? What was that?"

"I don't know. I don't know," he said.

"But you saw it."

"I saw it."

She turned to look out the driver's window again. There
was no sign of the Harpy. Just the forest floor, just the trees.

And then a giant rotting Cobra rose up beside the
window.

Molly was not given to panic. She was tough-minded—
and seasoned now, too, because she'd been through a lot.
But the sight of this uncanny thing seemed to set her mind
on fire. She screamed again and threw herself back toward
her dad, trying to get away from it.

The gigantic Cobra skull with its dagger-like teeth
jabbed at her, smashing into the window glass.

"Daddy, Daddy, what is it?" Molly screamed—she was babbling—she was that afraid.

But now the snake drew back and struck again and the window seemed to give and rattle in its frame. Another blow or two like that and the window might shatter or come loose and then the thing would be in the cab with her.

The fire of panic that had flashed in Molly's brain swept through and was gone. She was beginning to think again. A Harpy out of the sky. A giant rotting Cobra. This couldn't be happening. But it was. And she had to do something about it.

The Cobra drew back for another strike, rising up on its slithery coil of a body to get more leverage. Molly felt a wad of terror stuck in her throat. She couldn't believe what she was about to do. But she had to. She swallowed her fear. And she did it.

She grabbed the door handle. Cracked the door open. Waited.

"Molly, what are you doing?" her father said.

The Cobra struck.

Molly timed it perfectly. She threw the door open and smacked the snake hard in the face just as it darted at the window. Its head—which was mostly bone—went flying off, the top of the snake's spine exploding in a white blast. The rest of the Cobra's immense body spasmed and uncoiled and jerked on the ground. Purple lightning flashed through it. It sizzled. And in a purple blast, it was gone.

"Molly!" It was her father. "The compound!"

Still half crazed with fear and disbelief, Molly glanced at him. Her father had turned in his seat, was looking out his window at the side mirror there. Molly's mirror was gone, ripped off by the gate, and she couldn't get a good view of what was happening behind the truck.

But she could hear it. Shouting. The crackling of gunfire.

Without thinking, Molly threw the door open and jumped out of the truck to see what was going on. The glass of a broken headlight crunched under her sneakers.

"Molly!" her father shouted. "Get back in the truck!"

But she couldn't. She couldn't do anything but stand there, staring at what she saw.

An uncanny battle was going on at the compound gate. The soldiers there were battling a small army of impossible monsters. Giant Boar-like creatures wearing armor and wielding swords were hurling themselves against the soldiers' rifles. More Harpies were descending from the sky. More Cobras were slithering across the ground. All of the beasts were half rotten, their tattered flesh flying from exposed muscle and bone.

The soldiers loosed bullets at the attackers when they could. When the bullets struck home, the creatures reeled backward, shrieking. They fizzled and flashed with purple lightning and then pixilated into nothingness. But when the swords of the Boars or the talons of the Harpies or the fangs of the Cobras struck home, there was blood—a lot of it—and the soldiers let out wild cries of agony, horrifying for Molly to hear.

It was a moment before Molly could believe what she was seeing. It was another moment before she could figure out what to do. But she knew: She had to get out of here. She had to get Victor One to someplace where he could make contact with his friends. She had to bring help to the compound . . .

She heard her father call her name again from the truck's cab.

"We have to go!" he shouted at her.

She nodded. She turned to step back into the truck.

And as she did, there was a high, squealing shriek behind her.

She turned and saw a great Boar rushing at her on two legs. He had his sword raised in the air and was about to bring it down as hard as he could. Another second and it would cleave Molly's head in two.

20. BREAKOUT

RICK WAS IN the hospital when he heard the battle begin. He was locked in one of the secure rooms, a windowless cell. He was sitting on the edge of his cot, his hands held out in front of him as if he were begging. His eyes were lifted. He was gazing up into the rafters. He felt a new power pulsing through him . . .

They had locked him up in here after he'd come back from his near disaster in the Realm's seemingly eternal night—after Mars and the guards had arrested his father. Rick had been furious when they'd marched his dad away. He had threatened to rip Mars's head off. He had tried to do it too. It had taken the enormous Juliet Seven plus another guard to hold him back, to haul him out of the Portal Room, muscle him down the hall, and shove him through the door into here. He fought them every step of the way, shouting at Mars, calling Mars names, demanding Mars release his father, demanding he be allowed to see where his father was, to make sure he was safe . . .

Juliet Seven forced Rick through the secure room door

and shut it in his face. Rick heard the electronic bolt buzz into place, locking him in. He pounded on the door with his fists and went on shouting. He tried to kick the door open. He tried to pry it open with his fingernails. He shouted some more.

After a long while, the bolt was thrown back. The door opened. Miss Ferris walked in. She was carrying a stun gun, holding it up beside her head—in the safe position but ready to fire. The walking cement block that was Juliet Seven was right behind her.

"If you attack me, I'm going to have to knock you out," Miss Ferris said, her voice so flat she could have been reciting her grocery list.

Rick stood in the center of the room and glared at her. He wasn't going to attack her. She was half his size and a woman. But he wasn't afraid of her stun gun or Juliet Seven either. He felt angry enough to walk right through them both.

"Where's my dad?" he said.

"He's in another secure room. He's handcuffed to the bed, but he's not hurt. Mars is holding him on suspicion of treason."

"Mars is crazy. That's garbage. You know it's garbage. Mars has lost it."

Miss Ferris didn't answer. Rick couldn't be sure, but he suspected the strange little robotic woman agreed with him. Something in her eyes gave it away. It was nearly impossible to know, but it did seem there was something a bit more gentle and sympathetic in her voice when she spoke next.

"Right now," she said, "what we need is more information. We need to do some more tests on your brain."

"Forget it," said Rick.

"We need to know what just happened in there."

"It was dark. Black. There was nothing."

"Then where's Kurodar?" said Miss Ferris. "What's he planning? How did he get into Mars' computer?"

Rick was beginning to suspect the truth, but he wasn't going to tell it to Miss Ferris or to anyone until he'd had a chance to discuss it with his father. He just shook his head. "How should I know?"

"What did you see when you went into the Realm?" she asked him.

"I told you: Nothing. There's nothing in there anymore. It's just that blackness, that weird empty space that feels alive . . ."

Miss Ferris nodded once. "Then how did you get out?" she said. "If there was nothing—no portal—no passageway—how did you get back to RL?"

Rick didn't answer. The memory was only just beginning to return to him.

"Kurodar hasn't disappeared," Miss Ferris went on. "In fact, he seems to be reaching out somehow into RL. Someone killed the guard in the watchtower. Someone overrode the lock on Mars' computer. Something is wrong here, Rick; something is going on that we don't understand . . ."

"Well, it's not my father's fault," Rick said. "And Mars knows it too. He just doesn't like him, that's all. He's just looking for an excuse to get at him."

Miss Ferris blinked—which maybe indicated she was feeling some emotion or other. How could you tell? She lowered the stun gun to her side. Rick was glad. He didn't like being threatened, especially by the people on his own team.

All the while, Juliet Seven stood behind her, smiling. Rick thought he looked like he was hoping for a chance to tear him apart.

"Rick, you need to tell me something," Miss Ferris said. "Do you think it's possible that Kurodar is somehow . . . using your mind . . . that somehow while you were in the Realm, a connection was formed between the two of you?"

Again, Rick remained silent. That was exactly what he was afraid of.

Miss Ferris said, "Well . . . we can't let you out of here until we know more."

With that, she turned and left the room. Juliet Seven lingered just long enough to give Rick another of his smiles. Then he left too. When they were gone, Rick sat down on the edge of the bed. He put his head in his hands.

He thought about the blackness. Falling through the blackness. How *had* he gotten out? There was nothing to take hold of in there. No weapon. No portal point. Just that living blackness of Kurodar's imagination. How had he broken back into RL?

You won't go into your dreams alone . . .

He remembered his mother's words—and then he remembered everything.

It wasn't buried all that deep, not really. He remembered it all now: his terror . . . his spirit reaching out beyond the nothingness . . . his spirit calling across the darkness in a wordless prayer . . .

Rick lifted his head from his hands. He held his hands where they were, cupped in front of him as if he were begging. He lifted his eyes to the rafters.

That was the moment when Rick's faith finally came back to him, came back fully, came back strong. He had lost that faith when he lost faith in his father, when he lost faith in himself because the legs that had always carried him to victory on the football field were crushed and useless. But now he knew the truth. His father had never deserted him. The Traveler had had to make an impossible choice, an awful sacrifice, but it was a sacrifice made in love. Love was what the Traveler was all about. Because love was what his God was all about. And his God . . .

God had never abandoned Rick either.

Rick knew that now, knew it certainly, knew it in that way you know things when you don't need words for them anymore. He had never been abandoned. He had never been alone. And as for his legs . . .

His legs were not what they once were. They would never be what they were, never that reliable, never that strong, never again. He would never be the football player he'd wanted to be, the athlete he had dreamed of being. Never—and it hurt him in a way he could not have explained to anyone. To have his dream destroyed, to have his body compromised, it was a raging pain in his heart, even now, even still.

But now that he had seen the darkness of the Realm, the living emptiness of Kurodar's heart, now that he had been plunged into that blackness and come back alive, he knew the truth.

It was not his legs—it was never his legs—that had carried him to victory on the football field. Everything he needed for victory was still there, unbroken, untouched.

For the first time since that truck had hit him, Rick felt himself let go of his anger and his grief. For the first time in his whole hotheaded life, he was flooded with stillness and calm. He felt it flow up out of the core of him and through his limbs and into his mind like a golden liquid carrying a mighty power. For the first time in his life, he understood the source of his father's serenity. That Spirit that had answered his spirit in the darkness . . . That light of love no darkness could comprehend. That God of victory. His God.

Rick would never be the mighty Number 12 again. And it hurt. It would go on hurting for a long time. But the hurt didn't matter to him anymore. He could shake it off like a hard tackle. He was strong again, strong as the boy he once had been. Stronger. Strong as the man he needed to be.

Just then—that's when the noise of battle reached him. From outside, in the compound. Soldiers shouting. Gunfire. And then . . . squealing . . . shrieking . . . monstrous noises that Rick recognized at once . . . the war cries of the dead creatures of the Golden City . . .

Rick realized what was happening right away. Kurodar was invading the compound through the Realm. Through *him*. Through the portal that had somehow opened in his mind when he came through the Breach.

Rick got off the bed and went to the door. He tried the handle again. Rattled it. The door stayed locked.

The portal, he thought.

He remembered the darkness ripping open in the Realm.

The portal goes two ways.

He sent out another prayer—another wordless prayer that came from deep in his spirit. He focused on the door. On the lock inside the door.

Please, he thought. He knew he could not do this alone. The human soul alone is a place of darkness. He needed the power of that light.

Please.

He went on focusing on the lock inside the door. Using the power of the Realm inside him. Bringing his whole spirit to bear on the computerized mechanism that set the lock in place.

Please . . .

Suddenly, with a little inner jolt, he felt the logic of the lock's machinery come into him. Its codes and numbers were spoken into his mind in a high-speed voice that he understood without understanding.

He moved the numbers with his mind.

There was a buzz as the bolt miraculously drew back.

Rick pushed the door with a sort of experimental gesture—and yes, it swung open! He expected to find a guard on the other side. But all the guards were gone. They had run outside to join the fight.

Grimacing at the pain that flashed through his legs, Rick ran after them.

21. BATTLEFIELD

MEANWHILE, THE BOAR Soldier rushed at Molly, sword upraised. The edge of the blade was already descending as she willed herself to move. She spun to the side with athletic grace, turning in a full circle as the sword whisked at her through the air. She came out of the 360 facing the Boar just as the metal whispered past her head and smashed into the metal roof of the truck's cab.

The Boar was stunned by the impact, metal on metal. With the sword down, his face was exposed to Molly. She had a chance to strike out at him. Even thinking fast, she was smart enough not to punch him. His skin looked as thick and rough as a log, as bristly as a porcupine. She was pretty sure she'd break her smallish hand if she tried a direct blow. Instead, she made a fist and brought the edge of it swinging around sidearm like a big hammer. The hammer-fist struck the Boar full speed smack in his naked nose.

It was a good blow. It hurt him. It hurt him plenty. Molly could tell by the way he squealed. The Boar staggered back. He tried to steady himself, to steady his sword, to ready it for another strike at her. But he backed over something—a stone maybe or maybe just a spot of uneven ground. Whatever it was, the staggering Boar tripped over it and spilled backside-first to the dirt. As he hit the earth, he lost his grip on his weapon. The sword dropped with a dull clang.

On the instant, Molly rushed for it. She leapt over the Boar's thrashing pig feet, stooped down, and grabbed the sword's handle. The Boar went onto all fours, struggling to rise. Molly grabbed the sword off the ground and kept moving. The sword wasn't light. It weighed about ten pounds. But with all that adrenaline in her, Molly barely felt the weight of it.

The Boar got to his feet. Molly halted. She turned. The Boar rushed at her. Molly swung.

She braced her back foot on the forest floor and used her whole body to bring the big weapon around fast, like a baseball bat. Of course, it weighed about five times what a baseball bat weighs, but she was still able to get some speed into it.

Before the Boar could reach her, the edge of the blade connected with the side of his head. Molly grunted at the impact, but her grunt was drowned by the shriek of the creature. Molly squinted at the brightness of the purple bolts that went through him just before he disappeared with a last tremendous flash.

She let the point of the sword sink to the ground. She looked around her.

The battle at the compound gate continued. Harpies flew down on the harried soldiers. Boars rushed at them. And Cobras coiled up out of the earth and tried to strike at them. More soldiers had come running from the barracks to join the fight, but more and more monsters were materializing out of the earth and out of the air. The men and monsters battled back and forth at the entrance in the barbed-wire fence.

Molly knew she had to go, had to get out of here, had to get her father and Victor One to safety. She turned and took a step toward the truck.

But it was already too late.

Boars and Cobras were springing out of the ground all around her. Harpies appeared in midair and swept down on her.

In an instant she was surrounded by monsters.

22. LONE SOLDIER

MOLLY KNEW SHE was done for. The fight with the Boar had left her at a distance from the truck. In a moment—before she could move or even think—two giant Cobras sprang into being, cutting her off from the truck's door. When she turned—wherever she turned—left or right—the Boars were standing before her with their swords upraised. And even as she stood there, frozen in fear and despair, a gray, shrieking Harpy was descending on her out of the sky.

Molly decided if she had to die, she would die fighting. In that final second before the creatures closed over her, it was the only thing she could think to do.

She managed to raise the sword in time to run the point into the center of the attacking Harpy. The she-creature shrieked and flashed and vanished—leaving Molly free to swing again, blocking the blow of an onrushing Boar.

But already her strength was failing. The sword was growing heavy and her arms were growing weak. The clash with the Boar sent her staggering backward. The Cobras seized the moment to slither toward her. The Boars rushed at her. Another Harpy screamed and fell on her from the side.

Despite the weakness in her arms, Molly managed to swing the sword again—once, twice—forcing the snarling creatures back. But an instant later, her blade struck the blade of a Boar and she lost her grip on the weapon. The sword went flying out of her hands, fell to the forest floor, and vanished.

The Harpy came at her with a shriek. Unarmed, Molly let out a shriek of her own. She raised her hands, ready to fight with just her nails and teeth if she had to, but she knew it would make no difference. She knew the end had come.

The Harpy, its terrible face frozen in a cry of bloodlust and rage, rushed down at her, its razor claws sweeping through the air. Molly caught the thing by the throat with one hand. Caught the slashing arm by the wrist with the other. Hurled the beast into the Cobras, making their slithery, bony bodies dodge to the side, halting their advance.

Then the creatures charged and swept over her. She was overpowered. On instinct, she threw her hands over her head and fell to her knees, waiting to die.

A second passed. Another second. She felt the presence of the monsters all around her. She heard their growls and snarls and screams. But they didn't fall on her. She didn't die. She couldn't understand it.

Molly lowered her hands and looked up.

The mob of monsters was still there. They towered

over her. But they had turned away from her. She saw their backs—the backs of the Boars and the Cobras. They were all facing away from her. Even when another Harpy materialized out of the forest sky and swept down screaming, it did not sweep down on her.

The monsters were battling something behind them. Something—someone—had engaged them in a deadly melee. Molly watched, astonished, as first one, then another, then another of the creatures flashed purple and vanished. Even as new monsters rose up to take the places of the fallen, the ranks of the creatures began to thin. A few seconds more, and Molly could see through the mob to its center.

And there was Victor One.

He was a horrifying sight. His face was gray and green. His eyes were streaked with red. His old wound had opened and the front of his shirt was stained nearly black with blood. He had a piece of wood in his hand— one of the boards from the crates inside the truck. The board had nails sticking out of one end and V-One was using one hand to swing and jab with it expertly. With his other hand he grabbed and struck and slashed. The Boars fell at his feet. The Cobras exploded. The Harpies spiraled out of the air like crashing planes. Every second Molly watched, another of the creatures flashed and died and vanished under Victor One's assault.

"Get in the truck!" he shouted at her, never stopping his attack for a moment. "Get in the truck and go!"

Molly hesitated. She looked around her quickly. More monsters were springing out of the earth, materializing out of the sky. She hated to leave Victor One alone in this battle, but he was right: if she didn't move, she and her father would be swarmed and killed. If she could get the truck moving, maybe she could pull V-One on board and they could all escape together.

"Go, go, go!" he shouted.

Molly obeyed him. The Cobras who had stood in her way were gone. She leapt to the truck. She climbed into the driver's seat, pulling the door shut behind her. She wrestled the gear shift into neutral. She reached for the ignition. Would it start? It had to. It had to.

She hit the ignition. She hit the gas. The engine whined. It fought to engage. It coughed. But no . . .

She tried again. Again, it whined and coughed—and then, yes, it started!

But too late. Boars and Cobras continued springing out of the ground all around her. Harpies appeared in midair and dove at the windshield. In an instant the truck was surrounded with monsters, even as Victor One tried to fight them off outside.

Molly put the truck in reverse. She stepped on the gas. She tried to back through the attacking creatures. But they swarmed over the vehicle. They hit it hard. The engine sputtered and died again. The truck stopped still. The creatures hammered at it, rocking it back and forth. Cracks spider-webbed over the windshield. The driver's window began to cave in. Molly tried to start the truck again, but it wouldn't happen.

She looked at her father. He stared back helplessly. She looked all around her.

The creatures were everywhere.

23. RESCUE QUEST

RICK RUSHED TO the door of the hospital barracks and looked out. The scene in the compound was incredible to see. Monsters blooming out of the earth. Monsters flashing out of the empty air. Soldiers shooting at the creatures with rifles. Stabbing at them with bayonets and combat knives. But for each creature that fell to earth, shrieking and flashing and disappearing, another grew up in its place. New soldiers were charging across the compound to join the fight, but there were only so many of them, and the monsters might appear forever. Already, as Rick watched, the soldiers were falling back and the monsters pushing forward. Soon, the soldiers would be swarmed and overcome.

Rick didn't hesitate. Ignoring the pain in his legs, he started running. Somehow he had to stop this. Somehow he knew he could, knew that he was the only one who could. He didn't feel Kurodar using him as a portal, but that had to be what was happening. Nothing else made sense. The Realm was inside him now . . .

But it wasn't the only thing inside him. His spirit was

there and his spirit could control the Realm. He knew that. His spirit could control the shape of things there. If he could somehow take hold of the inner portal. If he could somehow close that portal down . . .

Rick drew near to the heart of the battle—so near that a Cobra sprang up beside him, baring the fangs in its skull, ready to strike. Rick struck first, with a huge round-house punch. His fist smacked full force into the side of the Cobra's head. The snake's black eyes went milky white. It dropped sideways to the earth. It flickered. Flashed. It was gone.

And Rick turned to the rest of them.

With the melee noisy and bloody all around him, it was no easy thing to bring his focus to bear. But that was part of who he was, what he could do. He went inside himself. He narrowed his attention to a pinpoint, like a beam of light. He looked deep into his own spirit . . .

And there it was. Hidden away in him, like a secret sin. He saw it now. The link to the darkness of the Realm that had somehow become lodged in his own brain, the passage that linked him to Kurodar's evil.

With all the force of his spirit, he willed the portal to close.

He could feel it happening. It was like the stone eye of a giant idol slowly shutting, the lid slowly lowering. He could not shut the gap forever, but he could shut it for now, hold it fast for a little while, at least.

With a sort of inner thud, it shut. He felt it.

And almost at once, he saw the monsters stop appearing. The ones who were already there remained, fighting the battle, but no more Boars and Cobras grew out of the ground, no more Harpies materialized in the sky. He had closed the portal.

With no more monster reinforcements, the harried soldiers of the compound began to turn the tide of battle. They fired their automatic weapons in short bursts. Harpies dropped out of the air, shrieking. Boars squealed and fell and died. Rotting Cobras exploded in blasts of white bone. Step-by-slow-step, the soldiers began to move forward, driving the creatures back against the fence.

Rick looked round him, searching for a weapon with which to join the fight. As he turned, he saw a commotion out beyond the compound, at the edge of the woods on the other side of the half-open gate.

A mob of dead, half-rotten creatures had gathered there. They were swarming over something. What was it? A truck. The monsters mobbed it, threw themselves at it, crawled over the top of it, attacked it again and again. They looked like ants devouring a sugar cube.

A truck . . . , Rick thought.

He felt something darken in his heart. Wasn't a transport truck coming to collect Molly and Professor Jameson this morning?

As the soldiers and monsters fought one another at the compound's perimeter, Rick began moving through the chaos. He went slowly at first, trying to see what was going on out in the woods, what was at the heart of that swarm of creatures out there. But as the thought of Molly kept coming back to him, his footsteps quickened. Soon he was running again, running toward the gate.

A fallen soldier lay on the ground in his path. Wounded, bloody, but still breathing, his arm was lifted to his face, the back of his hand resting on his forehead. His automatic rifle lay beside him in the dirt. The strap was broken and lay twisted in the dirt like a green snake.

Rick barely broke stride as he reached down and snapped the rifle up. He readied it to fire as he went on running toward the truck.

He came through the gate. He had a good view of what was happening now. The truck was damaged, stalled. It had obviously crashed into the nearby pine tree. He could see the damage in the tree's bark. There was glass on the forest floor and what Rick could see of the truck's fender was dented. Harpies and Boars and Cobras were hammering at the cab again and again, trying to break in through the windows and windshield. Harpies were tearing at the canvas that covered the flatbed in back. Some of the snakes were trying to slither in over the rear gate, but every time they tried, something beat them back.

It was another few steps before Rick could make out Victor One, battle-mad, blood-soaked, wildly swinging a two-by-four to keep the creatures off the truck.

But the Harpies were up above him, out of his reach. They were on top of the vehicle, shredding the canvas covering. Soon they would come through and attack the cab from the rear.

Rick raised the rifle chest-high and opened fire. He had to be careful not to hit the people in the truck so he aimed at the edges of the monster mob, and let off only a short three-bullet blast at a time. He went for the Harpies on the canvas first. The bullets tore into their gray, rotting flesh. The winged woman-like things flew back into the air, shrieking and sparking. One vanished midair. Another dropped writhing and flashing to the ground and then was gone.

Rick fired again. And again. A Cobra's head exploded. A Boar fell to the earth wounded. He pulled the trigger again—and nothing. A useless click. The magazine was empty, the bullets gone.

Rick tossed the gun away. The wounded Boar still lay on the ground, the purple bolts of lightning zigzagging through him. His sword lay beside him, shimmering with purple light. Rick rushed for the sword. Grabbed it. His energy recharged it. The purple lightning went out. The sword grew solid in his hand. He raised it above his head and let out a wild battle cry. He charged into the fight, swinging the blade.

Victor One heard Rick's cry; he saw Rick charge. His pale face broke into a ghastly grin. His arms seemed to gain fresh strength as he fought the creatures all around him.

Molly saw Rick come too. She had been fighting tears of terror as she tried to start the truck again. But now she let the ignition go and grabbed the door handle. As the Boars and Cobras launched themselves at her windows, she let out a yell and threw the door open and slammed it into them. Once, twice—sending two attackers flying. And as a Harpy tried to reach in and tear at her, she slammed the door on its clawed hand.

In the next moment, though, a Cobra hit the window and the glass caved in, the sharp, dangerous shards falling toward her. Molly reeled back in her seat, covering her face with her raised arms. When she looked again, the Cobra was right outside, ready to strike through the opening, through the space above the jagged shards in the bottom of the window frame. Its head darted in on her, its dagger-fangs bared. Its jaws snapped shut—just missing her as she leaned back desperately against her father. The Cobra began to withdraw for a fresh strike. Molly swallowed her disgust and launched herself forward. She used both hands to grab the thing. She slammed its head down onto the jagged glass. The Cobra let out a hissy gasp as the sharp shards pierced its underjaw. Molly saw the purple lightning flash inside it. Then it was gone.

Inspired by his daughter, cheered by Rick's charge, amazed at the courage and power of Victor One, Professor Jameson had taken up the fight as well. He wasn't exactly a warrior personality, but an old expression came into his mind—*Needs must when the devil drives*—which means, "When evil is on the march, you do what you have to do." He did what he had to do. He glanced at Molly. He saw her battle strategy. He threw his own door open with all his might and smashed a charging Boar in its pink nose. The Boar went down, but the window cracked and a large section of glass, smooth on one side and blade-like on the other, fell into the professor's lap. He picked the glass up with both hands and when a Harpy arced out of the air and came through the window at him, he jammed it into her shrieking face. Her claws scratched his arms painfully, but the glass destroyed her and she sparked and fell away.

Rick and Victor One were fighting side by side now. Rick felt himself filled with a weird furious superstrength, like Jonathan in the Bible when he attacked the Philistines single-handed or like Mega Man X when his charge meter is full. He was hacking through the mob of monsters as a scytheman carves through wheat. And V-One, who had gotten hold of a Boar sword himself now, was doing the same.

Cobras, Boars, and Harpies flew back and fell on every side of the two warriors. Monsters were lying all over the forest floor, purple lightning lancing through them as they twisted in their death throes before they disappeared. A final Boar came rushing toward Molly's window, its sword point lowered to deliver a killing thrust. It never reached her. Rick let out an animal roar and brought his own blade down atop the creature's head. Rick was so pumped with battle power that the edge of the sword cut all the way down to the Boar's collarbone before the thing vanished from in front of him.

The fight was almost over now. Victor One was slashing a last Harpy out of the air. Professor Jameson had stepped out of the cab to wield his glass shard more freely. There was only one Cobra left on his side and with a not-very-loud but heartfelt cry of "Take that!" he cut it down.

Rick reached the driver's door and pulled it open, and Molly poured out of it and into his arms. On the instant, the battle rage left his heart. He lowered the sword to his side and held her, glad beyond telling to feel her warm and alive. Until that moment, the fire of the fight had been burning so high in him he had not fully felt how frightened he was for her, how desperately he wanted to reach her. But he felt it now and held her close. His eyes looked past her and scanned the area. The monsters were gone. The battle was over. He let the sword fall from his hand. It dropped to the earth and vanished.

The battle in the compound was ending too. With a few final ragged volleys, the soldiers were killing off the last of the monsters there. Rick and Molly turned together, their arms around each other, and watched. A few final purple flashes and it was finished. The soldiers let up a brief cheer, their fists rising into the air. But the next second, they were racing over the frozen compound ground, picking up the wounded and carrying them toward the hospital barracks.

Professor Jameson came around the front of the truck to find his daughter. His always-disheveled self was even more disheveled than usual. His arms were running with blood from where the Harpy had scratched him. His shirt, stained with blood, was completely untucked. His slacks were filthy. He still held the glass shard he had used for a weapon in his hand. He said mildly, "Well, that was certainly . . ." Then he shook his head, unable to finish the sentence. The thick glass slipped from his fingers and fell to the forest floor.

Holding Molly, Rick turned to Victor One.

The bodyguard, pale and blood-soaked, was standing nearby under the trees. He swayed where he stood. He managed to show them a lopsided grin.

"I don't know what those things were," he said hoarsely. "But we kicked their butts back to fantasyland, that's for sure."

And with that, he collapsed to the ground.

Rick and Molly rushed to the fallen bodyguard and knelt beside him.

"Hold on, buddy, we'll get you help," Rick said.

But Victor One didn't answer him. He never spoke another word. He looked up—at Molly first and then at Rick—and he smiled at them. Rick's heart turned leaden and dropped inside him. He could see that V-One was leaving life behind.

Molly saw it too. Crying, she called out his name. She reached out and touched his face. Victor One went on smiling. He met Rick's eyes. He moved his head. It was only the faintest gesture, but Rick knew exactly what he meant.

He was telling him to take care of Molly: the girl they both loved.

Rick nodded. His throat felt so thick he could barely breathe. He wanted to speak but couldn't. He wanted to tell Victor One that he would defend Molly with his life—with his whole life and for his whole life. He wanted to tell him that he understood why V-One was smiling, why he was calm. He wanted to tell him that he knew now what Victor One knew, what the Traveler knew. He knew there was no fear faith couldn't conquer, not even this.

But there were no words for any of it. So Rick simply knelt there. A single tear spilled from his eye and ran down his cheek. Victor One tried to shake his head, to tell him there was no reason to cry, but he didn't have the strength. And it wouldn't have mattered. Rick's tear would have fallen anyway. He was heartbroken to see Victor One go.

Another moment and then the terrible thing came. A shadow seemed to move diagonally across the bodyguard's face. When the shadow had passed, Victor One was gone.

Molly moaned, "No," and turned away and pressed herself against Rick's chest. He held her there and she cried.

Rick held Molly and looked down at the body of Victor One. He hoped that Kurodar was still inside his mind. He hoped Kurodar could hear what he was thinking.

He was thinking: *I'm coming for you, Kurodar. I'm coming for you.*

He was going to destroy the Realm. There was no question in his mind. He was going to bring that weird and terrible universe down around Kurodar's head. He was going to bury the terrorist in his own rotten blackness. He was going to avenge Victor One.

It was another few seconds before Rick became aware of the shouting from the compound. He looked up and saw Mars.

The commander was standing at the compound gate with his silver hair unkempt, his face pale, one shirttail hanging out of his pants. He was pointing at them—at Rick and Molly and Professor Jameson.

He was shouting, "Get them! Arrest them! Don't let them get away!"

Already, a few of the soldiers were running out of the gate, running toward the truck, their rifles leveled.

24. HIGH TREASON

THE PRISONERS WERE brought into the underground conference room: Rick, Molly, and Professor Jameson all together, then the Traveler, blinking calmly behind his glasses and rubbing the place on his wrist where the handcuffs had been. The soldiers withdrew to guard the doors and the compound's medics came in. They cleaned the scratches on Professor Jameson's arms. They examined the bruise on Molly's forehead. They cleaned the cuts and bruises that Rick hadn't even realized he had sustained in the heat of the fight.

The conference room was a long room nearly filled by a long table. All along the wall were monitors and television and computer screens, all blank, all dark. Rick was standing at the head of the table. His father, the Traveler, was sitting in one of the swivel chairs positioned around the table's side. Rick had told him about the death of Victor One. The Traveler, who had become close to his bodyguard, had only nodded once then sat down silently, gazing at nothing. Rick knew he was silently praying for his friend.

Molly and Professor Jameson were seated too. The

professor held his daughter's hand. She had stopped crying for Victor One now, but her face remained drawn and sorrowful.

When the medics were gone, the prisoners looked at one another.

Rick smiled sadly. "You should've seen him," he said. "He must've killed fifty of those things all by himself."

"A hundred," said Molly softly.

"With a piece of wood and his bare hands. He was a warrior."

The Traveler nodded. "He was. He was a warrior through and through."

Molly and Professor Jameson nodded too. They all fell silent again.

A few more moments passed, then the conference room door opened. Commander Mars came marching in with Miss Ferris marching right behind him.

Rick's grief turned to a flash of rage at the sight of the man. For a second, he wanted to leap at him. He wanted to grab him by his lapels and scream in his face. He didn't. The second passed. His anger faded as he looked at Mars.

Mars looked awful. If the commander had seemed panicked before, he now seemed to have passed beyond panic to pure despair. The craggy face was pale and slack, as if the rock of the man's features had melted into something soft and putty-like. And his eyes—his eyes seemed distant, as if they were gazing on some scene of disaster that no one could see but him.

It was strange. Mars had been such a fierce and unyielding personality up till now. But it wasn't half as strange as what Rick saw when he turned to look at Miss Ferris.

Was it possible? Was even the Great Robot Lady of Robot World affected in some way? Yes, she was. There could be no question about it this time. Though Miss Ferris managed to keep that absolutely blank look on her face, she couldn't keep the fear out of her eyes. She couldn't stop her cheeks from turning ashen gray.

In the midst of his sorrow and anger, Rick realized that something terrible must be happening. If even Miss Ferris was feeling an emotion—any emotion—then whatever was happening, it had to be really big and really bad.

Mars spoke. And instead of his usual bark, his usual bullying style of command, there was a tone in his voice now of . . . what was it?

Humility, Rick thought. *Humility and fear.* Somehow Mars seemed to have discovered he wasn't as great as he thought he was.

"We have a situation on our hands," he said, and then he coughed. And then he said hoarsely, "A situation."

To Rick's surprise—to everyone's surprise—it was Molly who reacted first, reacted with a fury Rick had never seen in her. She let go of her father's hand and shot out of her seat. Her eyes flashed as she leaned toward Mars.

"A situation!" she said. "The situation is that you're a traitor."

"Molly!" said Professor Jameson.

"Dad, he is!" she insisted, never taking her flaming stare off Mars. "Victor One found out about him. That's why I was trying to smuggle him out of the camp. He found out that Mars used this entire project, the whole MindWar program, as a giant hack on America's defense systems. He stole the plans for a weapon system and was going to sell it to the enemy."

Rick slowly rose from his chair, staring at Mars, too, now. He could see by the look on the commander's face that what Molly said was true. It all made sense. That Battle Station thing he had seen in Mars's computer . . . That's why it was there. Mars had stolen the specs and was planning to sell them to the Axis.

Rick looked at his dad. The Traveler's reaction was subtle, but the son knew the father well. His dad's face remained serene, but the eyes behind the round glasses lost their mild aspect and went flinty and hard. He stood up too. He faced Mars.

"You were selling American secrets," he said quietly. It wasn't a question. It wasn't even an accusation. It was just a stated fact.

Mars couldn't meet the Traveler's eyes. He turned away. "It wasn't like that."

"Oh, what was it like?" Molly blurted angrily.

Rick could see Mars was trying to pull himself together,

trying to restore some semblance of his old authority and strength. It wasn't working. His cheeks were growing slick with sweat. His voice was still soft and hoarse.

"I was blackmailed . . . ," he said, his voice barely rising above a murmur.

"They were going to pay him a billion dollars," Molly said—and her voice sounded to Rick like steel clashing on steel.

Glancing at Mars, Rick could see that this was true as well. Mars—the great patriot!—had been going to sell a secret weapon for money.

"A billion dollars for the Battle Station specs," said the Traveler mildly. "You're a cheap date, Mars. They're worth ten times that."

"It wasn't like that," Mars said again, more forcefully this time. Rick couldn't tell whether he was trying to convince them or himself. "I thought I had an inside source with the Axis Assembly."

"Moros." Molly spat out the name.

Mars nodded. "I thought I had everything under control. I thought Moros and I were trading information. He told me some things, I told him some . . ."

"Like the fact that I was working on the MindWar Project," said the Traveler. "That's why they drove that truck into Rick. To get to me. That's why they broke into my house and held my son at gunpoint. That's how they knew where to attack my car on the road."

Mars nodded weakly, licking his dry lips. "By the time

I realized Moros was double-crossing me, it was too late. I'd already committed treason. He started to blackmail me. I had to give him more and more information or he'd have had me arrested, put in prison. And finally . . ."

"Finally you struck a deal with him," said the Traveler, his voice steady. "The Battle Station specs for the money."

"So I could get away. It wasn't the money, I just . . . I couldn't stand the idea of going on trial . . . for treason . . . prison." Rick was startled—everyone was startled—even Mars himself was startled—when tears came into the commander's eyes. He dropped his chin on his chest. He raised his hand to his face. "It wasn't the money . . . ," he said again.

There was silence in the room for a moment. Rick stood at the head of the conference table and looked at Mars—Mars with his head bowed, his hands to his eyes: a broken man.

Rick wanted to hate the guy. He felt he should have hated him. Mars's corruption had cost Rick the strength of his legs, his football career. It had nearly gotten him and his family killed. In fact, if it hadn't been for Mars, maybe Victor One would still be alive . . . Rick wanted to hate Mars and in the old days he would have. In the old days, he would have flown into a rage. But somehow, in the last few hours, those old days had ended. It was because of what had happened to him in the Realm. Because he had been into the very heart of the Realm's darkness. Because he had seen the light—the living, conscious light of love—that shone beyond it, that saved him when nothing else could. That light . . . somehow it had gotten inside him. It had begun to wash the hatred out of him. The hatred, the anger . . . It just wasn't there the way it used to be. Looking at Mars, Rick felt . . . Well, he felt a kind of pity for the man more than anything. Mars had been arrogant. Prideful. He had thought he could handle things alone. He had put his trust in himself. To use his mom's phrase, he had trusted his own brain. Big mistake. Rick felt pity for him, and the pity made him strangely calm. Calm, like his dad always was.

"Why are you here?" Rick heard himself say. He was really curious. He really wanted to know. "You weren't planning to confess like this. You were going to frame my dad so no one would suspect it was you. You must've been found out. They must be coming to arrest you." Mars lifted his face to look at him, his eyes still damp. Rick could see by the fear in those eyes that he was right. "Why didn't you run for it? Why are you still here?"

Mars straightened. He tried to put on the aspect of his former dignity. "I'm still a patriot," he said.

Molly gave an angry snort of derisive laughter.

"I am!" Mars protested. "I panicked when Moros blackmailed me. I gave him the specs to the Battle Station, but the Axis is years—decades—away from acquiring the technology needed to build it. By the time they got one up and running, we'd have come up with something more powerful. I never imagined . . ."

His voice trailed away. The room was silent.

"You never imagined what?" Molly snapped at him.

But Rick said nothing. The Traveler said nothing. They looked at each other. They had both already guessed the truth. The portal in Rick's head . . . Kurodar's hack of Mars's computer . . .

"Kurodar has taken control of the Battle Station," Rick said.

Mars answered nothing. He walked slowly, unsteadily, down the length of the long conference table until he was standing at the opposite end from Rick. There was a small black control panel there, with black switches in black plastic slots. He threw some of the switches. The monitors all along the wall lit up. On each big screen, there were animations of space . . . images of the sun . . . the earth . . . a depth of stars . . . And at the center of each screen was an animation of a satellite. Rick recognized it at once: it was the Battle Station, the space weapon he had seen on the specs in Mars's computer. He felt fear spreading through him like a mushroom cloud.

"Kurodar followed my computer straight into our defense systems," Mars said. "Straight into the controls of the weapon itself. Half an hour ago, the Pentagon alerted me . . ."

He stopped talking. His hand shook so hard he had to press it against his leg to still it. Everyone was looking at the massive floating space cannon turning around on the screen between earth and sun. Mars managed to reach for another switch in the panel, to draw it down. Next to each image of the station, a meter appeared, a long black bar that was only just beginning to fill with green light.

"He's using the sun to charge the station now," Mars said. "Within three hours, that bar will be full, the cannon will be operational." Mars raised his haunted eyes and looked at one and then another and then another of them.

"When that happens," he said, "Kurodar will be able to set the entire country on fire."

25. MISSION CRITICAL

SUDDENLY EVERYONE WAS talking at once. The Traveler, Molly, Professor Jameson, Mars, even Miss Ferris. Their voices were overlapping as they reacted to the news. Kurodar had control of the Battle Station. Three hours before it was operational. Three hours before the United States was in flames . . .

Only Rick was silent. He stood at the head of the table. He went on gazing at the screens along the wall, the images of the Battle Station, the earth, the sun. The meter filling with solar energy.

The same words kept echoing in his mind over and over: *Through me. He did it through me.*

"I have to go back into the Realm," he said quietly.

No one heard him. Molly was snapping accusations at Mars. Mars was defending himself. Miss Ferris was trying to get everyone to calm down. Professor Jameson and Lawrence Dial were discussing possible ways to break Kurodar's grip on the station.

"I have to go back into the Realm," Rick said again, louder this time.

Molly stopped talking midsentence and turned to him. Mars turned to him, then Miss Ferris. Finally, the two scientists ended their discussion and looked at Rick. The room was quiet.

Rick said it for the third time: "I've got to go back in. I've got to break Kurodar's interface. It's the only way we can stop him before the weapon charges, before he sets it off."

The others stared at him. For a moment, no one responded. No one said a word.

Then Miss Ferris said, "But . . . you can't. There's nothing there anymore. You said so yourself. The Realm is just blackness now. It almost killed you."

"The Golden City is still there," Rick told her. "I've seen it. Kurodar has let the rest of the Realm go dark and concentrated all his energies on the Golden City. For this. So he could do this."

Again, there was a moment of silence as everyone took in his words.

"But we have no portal in the Golden City," Miss Ferris said. "We've never established a presence there."

Rick looked into her eyes—those robot eyes that were now very human, very afraid. "I have a portal," he said. "I am the portal. I'm the passage Kurodar used to get into our systems. I can use that same passage to get into his. I've done it. I do it every night. All I have to do is go to sleep and I'm there."

"But . . . ," Miss Ferris began again.

Rick lifted a hand and she fell silent. "I can do it, Miss Ferris. I've got to do it. It's the only way to stop him."

Miss Ferris looked at him another long moment. Then she turned a questioning gaze to the Traveler.

Lawrence Dial nodded. "It could work. We give Rick a tranquilizer, put him to sleep . . . He might be able to control his immersion."

"I can control it," said Rick. "I'm sure of it."

"If you could," said his father quietly. "If you could get into the Golden City . . ."

"I can."

"If you could *destroy* the Golden City . . . it would sever Kurodar's interface. The Realm itself would collapse. And Kurodar . . . I have to think he's blended his brain so completely with his computers that he can't be separated from the Realm and live." He gazed thoughtfully at his son. "If you could do it, you could end this."

"No," said Molly. She had turned her fierce gaze from Mars to Rick. "No, even if you got in there, how would you destroy it? How would you even know what to do?"

Rick moved from the head of the table to stand close to her, to look down into her eyes. "I'm not sure, but I think there's a way."

Molly shook her head. "No," she said again. But then she said, "What way?"

"I met someone—in my dreams," Rick said. "In the Golden City. There's a . . . a sort of witch. Part of Kurodar's imagination. He doesn't want her there, but he can't help

203

it. She goes wherever his imagination goes. She told me I had to travel into the belly of the beast. She told me I had to face the horror Kurodar can't face . . ."

"But . . ." Molly went on shaking her head. Her eyes had turned soft and glassy now with a sheen of tears. "What does that even mean? Do you even know what that means?"

Rick had to admit it: "Not exactly. I'm not sure, but—"

"Not sure!" Molly said. "Dreams! Witches! You don't even know if any of it's real, Rick. You almost died last time. You can't just go in there and face . . . No one knows what . . ."

She stopped talking but went on shaking her head. And Rick went on gazing into her brown and urgent eyes a long time. He could not imagine why it had taken him so long to figure out he loved her.

"I've got to, Mol," he said finally. "I've got to go in there and destroy it. Not just part of it, all of it. For Victor One. For everybody."

"No . . . ," Molly whispered.

Rick glanced up at the Battle Station on the monitors. The energy bar slowly filling. He turned back to Molly. The sight of her made him ache.

"One last time," he promised her. "One last time."

26. DOORS OF THE MIND

THEY WERE IN the deepest part of the compound's underground complex now. The two glass portal coffins stood in the center of the room. In one coffin lay the body of Fabian Child—the Army clerk who was trapped in the Realm as Favian. In the other coffin was the blinking black box that held the Mariel program. A cot had been placed between them.

Rick lay on the cot. His sleeve was rolled up, his arm bare for the injection. A plastic monitor strip had been wrapped around his brow, colored lights blinking on it. It would project images from his mind into the compound's computers.

The computer screens and keyboards and servers were arrayed all around the walls. Some of the screens showed images of the Battle Station turning in space, its power bar filling. Others showed Rick's vital signs. Some were blank, ready to project images of the Realm when Rick got inside. Techs had crowded into the place to monitor Rick's progress. Lawrence Dial and Professor Jameson both had seats before keyboards and screens.

Molly stood at Rick's side, holding his hand. Miss Ferris was next to her, a gleaming steel tray beside her. It was the sort of tray you see in a hospital operating room. There were glass vials and syringes laid out on it. Miss Ferris was stone-faced as she fed the chemicals in one vial into a syringe.

Mars wasn't there. He had slipped away at some point. No one knew where.

"All right," Miss Ferris said, squirting a little fluid out of the syringe to clear any air in there. "This should relax you."

Rick smiled wryly with one corner of his mouth. "Nothing's going to relax me," he said. Funny that he could smile and joke with his stomach in such a knot. "Just knock me out, that's the idea. Get me to sleep and I'll do the rest."

"Now that I know who Fabian is," the Traveler said, nodding toward the glass coffin that held the Army clerk, "I'm going to try to program a new portal designed for him specifically, taking into account the damage he suffered: that's what locks him inside. I'm going to try to inject the new portal into the Realm through your mind. With luck, it should appear wherever you are."

Rick glanced at him, nodded. "Do your stuff, Dad," he said. "I promised I'd get him out, so make it happen."

"As for Mariel . . . ," the Traveler began. But then his voice trailed off.

Rick understood. "Just help me get Favian out of there. Mariel . . ." He glanced at Molly. "Mariel's just a computer program. She doesn't know it, but we do. There's no point bringing her out. She's not alive, she can't die."

His dad nodded. He knew that wasn't exactly the way Rick felt. Whatever Mariel was in RL, in the MindWar Realm she was noble and beautiful. She had been Rick's guide and protector every moment he was in that dreadful place. She had armed him and guided him and given him hope. Rick would gladly have risked his life to save her . . . but there was no one there to save.

Professor Jameson looked at a clock on a control panel. "We've only got two hours and forty-five minutes left . . ."

Rick glanced at Miss Ferris. She nodded. "I'm ready."

Rick looked up at Molly. Molly squeezed his hand and tried to smile. "I'm ready too," she said.

Rick let out an unsteady breath. "Then let's do this."

Miss Ferris approached him with the syringe. Rick didn't look at her. He just went on looking up at Molly. If this was the last time he ever saw RL, he wanted her face to be the thing he remembered. If he was trapped in the slow, near-eternal death of the Realm, he wanted to be able to picture her for as long as he could.

He felt Miss Ferris swab his arm. He felt the needle press against his skin. He felt a drop of water: Molly's tear falling from her cheek onto his.

He smiled up at her. "Let not your heart be troubled," he said. He glanced over at his father, seated by a monitor. "That's how it goes, right, Dad?" He did not know his Bible the way his father did, the way Victor One had.

But the Traveler nodded. "That's exactly how it goes. 'Let not your heart be troubled, neither let it be afraid.'"

Rick nodded up at Molly. "Neither let it be afraid," he repeated.

Miss Ferris inserted the needle into his arm and pressed down on the syringe plunger, flooding his vein with sedative.

"Neither let it be . . . ," he began again, but his voice faded. He felt sleep washing down over his eyes like a liquid curtain. Molly's face swam above him and started to sink away from him. He wanted to tell her he loved her one more time, but he couldn't get the words out.

Darkness.

Then, seconds later, he was in the worst nightmare of his life.

BOSS LEVEL: THE KING OF THE DEAD

27. WITCH'S WISH

HE STOOD ON the edge of the valley of death. It seemed to stretch out before him forever. It was bizarre: There was no color to it. It was like one of those old black-and-white movies his mom sometimes watched on TV. On every side, the stony ground stretched out in shades of gray. And everywhere, in shades of gray, lay the bodies.

Of course. This was how he had exited the Realm last time, so this was the only way back in: through the visions of Baba Yaga's table. The millions—the tens of millions—of people murdered by the Soviet Union, the country—the empire—of Kurodar's father.

Rick looked around him at the dreadful and macabre scene.

They wanted to make the world a paradise, the Traveler had told him.

Pride, Rick thought. *Like with Mars.*

He wanted to turn away from what he saw. He wanted to turn back—turn back to the room in the underground MindWar complex where his friends were waiting for him. It was horrible to be trapped in this netherworld between his own brain and Kurodar's buried memories. He wanted to get out of here now.

But he couldn't. Somehow, he had to make his way across this endless, hideous plain of corpses. Somehow, he had to return to the chamber of Baba Yaga. Back to Favian. Back to the Golden City.

He hesitated one more moment. He didn't like to step out among the bodies, but he knew he had to. He took a deep breath. He started walking.

The moment he made that choice, things changed. The scenery around him began—eerily—to move on its own. The black-and-white scenes began to speed back past him, like scenery through a car window. As he continued to walk, the scenes sped up, went even faster until they were going by in a blurred rush. Rick felt as if he were suddenly falling through this landscape of death . . . but weirdly, instead of falling down, he was falling up.

He lifted his eyes in the direction of his fall. Somewhere up there beyond the black and white, a splash of color appeared. It was a dark color, brown streaked with shadows, almost indistinguishable from the grays of the hideous scene. But Rick's heart rose when he saw it. He knew it was a way out of this terrible Soviet tableau.

The scene rushed past him. The brown gateway grew closer. Soon he heard the soft echoing sound of witchy laughter—in the distance at first, but growing louder, nearer. He began to make out shapes . . . A gleaming white light . . .

Then, the next thing he knew, he found his own shape becoming insubstantial—a sparkling thing like Favian. The high, witchy laughter echoed louder and surrounded him. The gateway spread around him like the open mouth of a monster ready to swallow him. There was a sort of *swoosh*, and suddenly, he was through the gate. He was back again in the last place he had been, back in Baba Yaga's chamber, back beside the crystal table, standing in its eerie white glow, while the witch reeled back from the tabletop and laughed and laughed and laughed.

Rick fought to catch his breath.

I made it, he thought.

He had come through the portal in his brain. He was back inside the Realm.

Baba Yaga went on laughing at him, rocking back and forth in her chair. The warts on her face grew whiter as her greenish cheeks grew red. Her malevolent eyes sparkled.

Dazed, Rick's hand went instinctively to his side. He felt the handle of Mariel's sword in its sheath there. His fingers closed around it, and Mariel's presence and power seemed to flow through him, clearing his mind.

He turned to his side. Favian was standing there—just standing, absolutely still—standing and staring into the light of Baba Yaga's table as if hypnotized. His blue and shimmering light-form was exactly as it had been the moment Rick fell into the witch's visionary table. Even the look of worry was still there on the sprite's face.

"Favian? Are you all right?" Rick said.

"He's fine! Fine, fine, fine," the old crone cackled. "I put him in a sleep, that's all, so he would be here when you came back."

He's been asleep all this time? Rick thought—but even as he thought it, Baba Yaga suddenly stopped laughing and lifted her wrinkled hands and waved her crooked fingers in the air. At that, Favian blinked and straightened and came to, looking around him, dazed.

"Rick!" he said, his voice cracking with delight as he spotted his friend. "You're back!" Judging by the look of relief and wonder in his eyes, he hadn't expected to see Rick ever again.

Rick grinned. "Don't sound so surprised, man."

"Well, I thought . . . It was like you turned to light and just *swooshed* right into the table and I thought . . ."

"Not even a problem," said Rick, with way more cool than he was feeling. "Show a little faith, you know?"

"Yeah. Faith. I was never very good at that. Anxiety is more my thing. I'm great at anxiety."

"Enough," said Baba Yaga in her creaky voice. She rubbed her hands together. "There's no time for chitchat and camaraderie. A great calamity is coming, greater than anything that has come before."

Rick nodded at her. "I know. It's coming to RL too. I came back here to try and stop it."

"I've given you what I can. You have the knowledge now. If you use it in time, you can end this place forever."

Favian's eyes went wide at that. He shimmered where he stood like a blue summer dusk. "But . . . But if the Realm dies . . . I die . . . I have nowhere else to go."

Baba Yaga shrugged as if it didn't matter to her whether Favian lived or died.

But Rick assured him, "Not gonna happen, buddy. You and I are getting out of here together. My dad is building a portal for you right now."

He spoke the words as confidently as he could, and he was glad to see a small flare of hope appear deep in Favian's eyes.

"Really?" the blue man said.

"Hey, my dad could program a computer to tap-dance and whistle 'Dixie.' He wrote the programs that got us all in here in the first place, so believe me, if anyone can get us out again, he can."

"That's great," said Favian. "Mariel always said you'd free us from this place."

Rick pressed his lips together. Without thinking, his fingers closed around the sword hilt at his side again. What could he say to that? Mariel had been the only friend and companion Favian had had here. There was no point telling him that she was just a bunch of code: a brain dub—or what had his father called it?—a "connectome" of one or more of the volunteers the Traveler and Professor Jameson had used. Here, in the Realm, Mariel was every bit as real as they were. Back in RL, she was just a black box spitting out numbers. How could he tell Favian that the wonderful water woman would cease to exist the moment the Realm did? How could he even begin to explain that?

Rick reached out and put a reassuring hand on Favian's shoulder—or what would have been a reassuring hand on what would have been Favian's shoulder if Favian had been a person of flesh and blood. As it was, he was more a sort of living light show, and all Rick felt when he touched him was an electric tingle against his palm.

"Enough!" screaked Baba Yaga again. "You must go. You must find the center of the city!"

Rick looked at her. He didn't know whether to trust her or not. Why would she want to destroy this place in which Kurodar's childhood memories kept her alive? And yet, for some reason, he believed she wanted to be free of the Realm as much as Favian. He sensed the yearning in her—her wish to get out of Kurodar's imagination even if it meant the end of her existence.

"What do we do?" he asked her.

Baba Yaga leaned over her glowing table and made a few more eerie passes with her gnarled fingers. She peered into the light as if she could see the future there . . . though Rick had seen only Kurodar's memories of horror and bloodshed.

"Find the silver one," she murmured, her voice like a creaking door. "She will take you where you need to go."

"Mariel," said Favian.

"Where can we find her?" Rick asked.

"There's water in the dining hall." She lifted a long, bent, warty finger, pointed at the door. "Below."

Even as she spoke, her voice became an echo. Her figure grew transparent, then dim. She started to fade away.

Just before she vanished, Rick heard her say, "But beware Bagiennik! He is trapped here, too, like me."

"Bagi-who?" said Rick.

But it was too late. She was gone.

"Oh, great," said Favian. "We don't even know what we're supposed to beware of."

But Rick softly echoed Baba Yaga's word: "Enough." And he turned away from the glowing table and strode to the door. He pulled it open. Before he could step outside, there was a blue flash and Favian was there in the hall in front of him. Startling the way he kept doing that. By his faint shimmering blue light, Rick saw the spiral staircase winding down and down. He paused on the landing and listened for noises from above.

"The banging's stopped, at least," he said.

It was true. When he'd left, the dead guardians of the Golden City had been pounding at the door above, trying to break through and come after them. But now the staircase was quiet and Rick realized . . .

Of course. Kurodar had redirected the monsters to invade the compound in RL. He could create more, but that took time and he was distracted with charging the Battle Station for his next attack. Maybe, Rick thought,

217

maybe he and Favian wouldn't have to fight their way over every street in the Golden City. Maybe they could get to the core fast.

He could hope, anyway.

"Let's go," he said.

And with a flash, Favian started down the stairs. Rick followed after.

————

In RL, meanwhile, the Traveler was hard at work. Seated in the underground chamber in an old office swivel chair, he pounded at his keyboard. He glanced at Professor Jameson seated at the station beside him. "I've started a scan of Fabian Child's avatar. If I can figure out the code change that's got him locked inside, I can make a new portal for him."

The large, hulking Professor Jameson nodded as he tapped away at his own keyboard. "I'm going to scan Mariel's connectome," he said. "If there's similar damage in each code, we should be able to compare it and isolate the equations."

The Traveler nodded and both went on typing silently.

Molly, meanwhile, remained where she was, holding Rick's hand as his body lay sleeping. She lifted her gaze and passed it over the monitors around the room. She saw images of the Battle Station, its power bar filling slowly. She saw waves and graphs wiggling and jumping. She saw white numbers pouring over black screens. She was an athlete, not a tech. She didn't understand a lot of what she was looking at. But she had that nonscientist's trust that science-types could do all sorts of magical things, so she hoped everything was under control.

Now her eyes moved to another computer. A thin Asian guy with enormous glasses on his small head was sitting at the keyboard. On the monitor, there were images that reminded Molly of old-fashioned video games she had seen on YouTube. Like *Space Invaders* or the first *Super Mario* or something like that. When the tech moved his head, Molly caught glimpses of the images reflected on his large lenses.

The Asian guy sensed her looking at him and glanced at her. "Hey," he said. "I'm Chuck." He was very young, not much older than Molly. He had a kindly smile.

"Molly," said Molly, with a small smile back at him. She gestured at the monitor. "Is that the Realm?" she asked him. "Is that where Rick is?"

"That's him right there," said Chuck, pointing to a pixilated white figure of a man. It didn't look like Rick particularly, but Molly immediately felt her heart squeeze in her chest at the sight of him, just as if it were Rick she was looking at.

"It's pretty primitive imaging, I know, only eight-bit," Chuck said. "But it's tough to read things directly out of someone's brain. We should be able to see what he's doing, anyway. Right now, he's in some sort of stairwell. And he's on the move." The tech worked his keyboard. The scenery on the screen shifted to follow the figure who was Rick—and another blue figure nearby him. "That's Fabian Child," said Chuck. "He's cut off from his living memory so he calls himself Favian in the Realm."

Molly peered hard at the screen. She watched the two primitive eight-bit figures descending a cartoon of a winding stairway down into darkness.

"It really does look like an old video game," she said.

"Well, I guess it is kind of like a video game," said Chuck. "Except, you know . . ."

"Except just the opposite," said Molly. "In a video game, you can die a hundred times, but you only have to get it right once. In the Realm you can get it right a hundred times, but if you die once, it's game over."

"Right," said Chuck. "Kind of like real life."

28. KILLER PLANTS FROM OUTER SPACE

IT WAS A long way down the stairs, but with the glowing Favian leading the way, they reached the bottom quickly. Now a dark corridor stretched out before them. Rick could see only a few feet ahead. Favian raised his hand and made a light emanate from his palm. At the end of the hall, a door came into view. Favian glanced at Rick. He looked worried. Well, what else was new?

"I don't know where we are anymore," Favian said. "Anything could be on the other side of that door . . . Maybe we should turn back and . . ."

"No," said Rick. "This was where the witch told us to go. And Mariel's close. I can feel her."

His hand was on the hilt of Mariel's sword again, the twined metal rising to her image. And it was true: he could feel her presence more strongly than before. This was the right way. This was where they were supposed to be. Whatever was on the other side of that door . . .

He nodded once at Favian and then went ahead. Favian, worried, hung back, floating just above the floor, holding out his palm to light Rick's way through the darkness.

Rick reached the door. He pressed his hand against it. He drew a breath. So far, everywhere he had been in this world, there had been dead, half-rotten security bots— discarded creatures of Kurodar's deteriorating imagination. Everywhere he had gone, he'd had to fight for his life.

He pushed the door open, ready for the onslaught.

But there was nothing. Quiet. An empty room.

They stepped—or, that is, Rick stepped and Favian flashed—into a long dining hall. Rick could see at once that that's what it was. Small windows very high on the walls, just beneath the towering ceilings, let in thin, gray, sickly beams of light from the world above. Rough wooden tables were everywhere and heavy chairs, some upright, some overturned, some broken into pieces as if someone had smashed them into the ground. On the tables—and on the floor—there were pottery plates and drinking vessels, whole, chipped, and shattered.

There's water in the dining hall, Baba Yaga had said.

Yes. Against the wall were large basins, filthy, with grimy plates in them and water spigots hanging over them. If only those spigots were still working . . .

For another moment, Rick and Favian stood shoulder to glimmering shoulder, looking around. It made no sense, of course, that there should be a dining hall in the Realm. Why should code-created security bots have to eat and drink? But by now, Rick understood: sense didn't matter here. The imagination had rules of its own. You can't imagine something you've never seen and, in fact, everything you imagine is assembled from things you have seen and experienced in Real Life. Only God makes stuff out of nothing, the rest of us cobble together variations on the work God's already done. So Kurodar's Golden City was cobbled together from cities he had seen and fairy-tale places he'd read about. There was night and day though there was no sun. There were beasts and witches from storybooks and games. And now there was a dining hall for creatures who didn't need to eat. That's just how it was.

Favian gasped. "Look . . ." His whisper was tense with anxiety—but, then, he was pretty much always tense with anxiety. "Over there, by the wall."

Rick had to step deeper into the room to see what Favian was pointing at, but then he did—and he grew tense with anxiety himself.

Against one wall lay the body of a dead . . . something or other. It was like nothing Rick had ever seen before. All he could tell by looking at it was that it was fearsome and disgusting. It was green and brown and had a huge sort of human figure, but long-bodied and with a sort of reptilian face. It seemed to be made out of old vines and leaves and plants, its long torso thin and twined and twisted, its arms and legs the same. To Rick, it looked like a half-creature half-plant that had grown organically out of the mold and filth that was collecting on the floor.

"Do you think that's Bagin . . . whatever she said? The thing we're supposed to beware of?" asked Favian.

"Maybe," said Rick.

"Maybe it's dead," Favian whispered with faint hope.

"Maybe," said Rick. "But I'm not sure that matters much. If Kurodar realizes we're here, he can bring it back to life quickly enough."

Seeing the beast, his hand had gone instinctively to the hilt of his sword again. And as his fingers touched Mariel's image, he felt such a surge of spirit and power go through him that he looked around the room again, startled, expecting to see her standing there in front of him.

He panned his gaze over the basins against the walls. There were two against the long wall to the right—the monster was lying between them. There were three more basins against the long wall opposite. All the basins were long, as large as bathtubs and as filthy as if they had not been cleaned in decades. Broken and unwashed dishes and drinking vessels cluttered them. And there . . .

Rick held his breath so he wouldn't make a noise. Whatever that thing was growing out of the floor, he didn't want to risk waking it up. Instead of talking, he glanced at the anxious face of Favian and lifted his chin toward the basin in the corner. Favian turned to look—and now he saw it too.

One of the spigots over the basins was leaking. Dripping.

"Water!" Favian whispered.

"Shh," said Rick.

Glancing at the green vine monster to make sure it was still lying motionless and dead, Rick began to shuffle slowly toward the basin with the dripping spigot. Every few steps he took, Favian would flash and catch up to him—and then let him go ahead again.

Rick reached the edge of the basin. It was so dirty that it was stained brown-red and even black in places. For a moment nothing happened. Then . . . drip . . . a drop of the Realm's silver water, stained brown and ugly, fell from the spigot into the basin's drain. Drip, drip. Two more drops.

Rick stared at the spigot. Slowly, slowly, another drop of water began to form on the lip of it.

Rick leaned toward the droplet. As softly as he could, he whispered, "Mariel? Are you there?"

And suddenly, there was a gargling roar behind him! Favian let out a shout. Rick spun round, clutching his sword.

The green beast was rising, coiling vine-like up off the floor, its globular eyes open, staring balefully, its long, twisted arms uncoiling out in front of it like a plant grow-ing in fast motion. It let out another gurgling roar.

With a sting of metal, Rick drew his sword. Too late. On the instant, the beast reached for him. One viny arm wrapped itself around the silver blade and yanked the weapon out of Rick's hand.

"Rick!" Favian shouted.

The blue sprite tried to send a blast at the advancing beast, but he was low on energy and only a pale light pulsed out of his palm. With casual brutality, the creature swiped at Favian with one unraveling arm. The viny appendage went right through the shimmering blue light of the sprite, but all the same, Favian was swept off his feet and thrown across the room.

Now the plant creature came straight at Rick. He was unarmed and tried to dodge out of its path, to get away. But the beast was too quick. Its arms stretched out on either side and branches swiftly crackled out of the main limbs, spreading like a thorny curtain that blocked Rick's way.

The green beast came at him with a strangely organic wavering motion. As the screen of branches folded around him, there was nothing Rick could do but back up—and soon, he couldn't even do that. His back hit the basin behind him and he was pinned in place between the basin and the advancing vine beast.

The long snout of the creature extended toward Rick's head and—woof!—what a stench it had, like something that had been rotting at the bottom of a swamp for a hundred years. Rick recoiled as the thing's neck undulated out toward him, as the sinister yellow eyes in the lizardly face widened in hunger, and as the long snout of the creature opened, showing yellow-white teeth that dripped with mire.

"I am Bagiennik!" the creature said in a deep, watery voice. The stink washed over Rick with its breath. "And I devour you."

And with that, it reared up, ready to snap down and bite Rick's head off.

Which is exactly what it would have done, except that now there was noise of a fluid eruption at Rick's back, like a geyser blast or the roar of a waterfall. Plates and pottery flew out of the basin, spun across the room, and dropped to the floor, shattering. Desperate, Rick looked straight up and saw her—Mariel—flowing into the air out of the basin's spigot.

She was towering. She was silver and majestic. Her beautiful and regal face was set in the stern expression of a queenly warrior.

As Bagiennik's open snout lunged at Rick's face, Mariel's mercurial hand snapped out and caught the monster by the throat. Rick drew back against the basin as far as he could, staring at the creature as it writhed horribly in Mariel's grasp, as it choked and gagged, its plant-like tongue extending out beyond its murky fangs.

Bagiennik struggled. It tried to writhe free. It tried to snap out at the silver shape of the woman who held it fast. But she, without flinching, reached her other hand right into the range of the twisting, biting head and wrapped her powerful fingers around its striving snout. She held its mouth shut. And as Rick stood pinned against the basin, Mariel, reaching over his head and holding the monster's head and neck in her two hands, suddenly pulled her hands apart in a mighty tearing motion.

Bagiennik gave a high, gurgling squeal, and the next thing Rick knew, the monster's head was gone—utterly gone—and a rain of dead leaves and twigs was showering down over him. The room filled with the horrible swampy stench of the beast. The bulk of its body—its long, viny form—squirmed back down into the muck on the floor. There, it instantly turned brown and rotten, the green stuff fluttering off it.

Finally, all that was left of the beast lay still and dead.

———

In RL, Molly saw the whole thing played out by pixilated eight-bit figures on Chuck's monitor. She saw the figure that was Rick pinned by the horrid yet cartoonish green monster that attacked him.

"What is that?" she said, her voice catching.

"Security bot," said Chuck.

"It looks like some kind of plant monster."

Lawrence Dial and Professor Jameson both looked up from their keyboards. "Bagiennik," the Traveler said. "Another creature out of Russian fairy tales. A plant monster, as you say."

Molly stared at the screen. She cried out, "It's got him! It's going to kill him!"

But the next moment, she saw the silver female figure rise gracefully up behind Rick. She knew at once who it was.

"Mariel!" she said.

Everyone in the room stopped what they were doing to watch the screen as the battle played out to its conclusion. A few moments later, Bagiennik was dead.

Molly hadn't realized she was holding her breath in suspense—and clutching Rick's hand tightly—but now she let the breath out and loosened her grip.

"That's good," said Chuck on a long sigh. "They're all together again. I always feel better when Rick finds Mariel and Favian. They make a good team."

Molly nodded, watching the figures moving together on the monitor. She was glad Rick had been rescued—of course she was—but though she didn't like to admit it to herself, she felt a twinge of something else as well. She knew it was beneath her—she felt it was wrong—but she couldn't deny the pang of jealousy that went through her. Rick had not told her everything about what happened to him in the Realm, but she understood enough. She understood that Mariel had helped him and protected him and taught him things, and she knew that he had feelings for her—feelings so strong they had almost taken him away from her. The woman, it turned out, wasn't real. But still . . .

Molly shoved the thought out of her mind, squelched the hot pang. Enough.

Just let her keep him safe, she prayed.

The three figures, white, silver, and blue, moved together across the screen.

Molly nodded to herself. She turned from the monitor to look down at Rick's sleeping figure. He seemed almost peaceful.

Keep him safe, she thought again.

With a sigh, she lifted her eyes.

That was the first time she noticed that Miss Ferris had left the room.

29. ARMORED CORE

RICK STAGGERED BACK and looked up at where Mariel hung in the air above him. Her silver form gave off no light, but the pale beams that came through the window were reflected on her, played over her, and made her gleam. Her face was still set in warrior mode, bold and serious. And Rick felt—what he always felt when he saw her—a surge of emotion he couldn't name. There was something about her—some combination of kindness and strength and majesty that moved him to his core.

But that feeling, the admiration he felt for her, was complicated now, wasn't it? Complicated by the fact that she wasn't what she seemed. She wasn't even a person at all, just a web of numbers downloaded from a human mind or some random combination of human minds . . . a computerized image destined to die when the Realm died.

But as long as he was here with her, it didn't matter. She was real.

"You saved my life," he said. He nodded to where the dead plant beast lay in the corner of the room. Shreds of leaf and wood were still drifting slowly down to the floor from where Mariel had ripped the thing apart.

Mariel looked down at him and he saw again the care and tenderness in her eyes—and felt it again too. "We can't let you die quite yet, Rick," she said gently. "After all, you're the only one who can free us from this place." She added, "Though, until you do, you might want to hold on to that sword I gave you."

With that, Favian flashed to his side. He held out his two shimmering hands and the silver sword seemed to float an inch or so above them.

Rick took hold of the sword's hilt—the image of Mariel—and let out a breath as the force of her spirit surged through him again.

The only one who can free us . . . , he thought guiltily.

If she only knew the truth. She still thought she was the avatar of a human being. How could he ever tell her?

He sheathed the sword. He looked at his friends. He could see on both their faces the strain and lines of effort and rapid, unnatural aging that were already beginning to show again. Stuck here in the Realm, they could not recharge their energies. They were constantly fading and weakening, sinking inevitably toward the Realm's horrible living death. A few times, Rick's dad had programmed some reinforcement energy into Rick's avatar so he could revive them. But there'd been no time for that on this immersion.

Well, that didn't matter, Rick thought. In a few hours,

they would be either out of here for good . . . or dead. Rick and Favian would be out of here, anyway . . .

He felt the surge of guilt again, but he forced it out of his mind.

"What's wrong, Rick?" Mariel asked him. She sensed his trouble.

He wanted to tell her the truth, but he felt the pressure of the passing seconds. With each tick of the clock, the Battle Station was charging. He had to get going. He said, "RL's in danger. Kurodar has taken control of a weapon. He can use it to set our entire country on fire."

Mariel inclined her head in a single nod. "I knew there was something going on. He's been moving to protect the Golden City with all his strength."

"What do you mean? Like, how?" said Rick.

"There's something happening in the center of the place, the interface," Mariel said. "I can't see what it is. There's a protective cloud. But there are flashes that light the interior. I've caught glimpses of what's in there . . . and what I've seen isn't good. There's something on the other side of the fog. Something big. Another security bot Kurodar's created to protect the place. But this one's different from the others somehow. It seems directly connected to Kurodar himself, a living outgrowth of his mind. What I mean is: it seems not only to be a security bot, it seems to be able to create other security bots out of itself, as if it were an extension of Kurodar's imagination." She looked down at him with her soft gaze. "I'm not sure even you can fight him, Rick."

Rick smiled a little. *Even you.* He was touched by her faith in him. Touched—and, again, guilty, because he knew he could not be the hero she'd been waiting for, the one who would save her. No one could do that.

Mariel seemed to read his mixed emotions. He felt her gentle, understanding look cut right through him. How could a woman who was so . . . so *womanly* . . . just be some kind of black box full of numbers?

"But if anyone can defeat this thing, I know it's you," she told him.

"Mariel . . . ," he blurted out. He had to tell her. It couldn't wait. He had to tell her the truth right now.

But she lifted a silvery hand to silence him. "We can't waste time talking now, Rick. You know I'll help you any way I can. Let me begin with this . . ."

It seemed then that Mariel wavered before his eyes, her silver form cascading downward like a sheet of water. In the next moment, the strange warmth of her seemed to pour over him, head to toe. When Rick looked again, she was still hovering in the air above him, but she had grown paler, weaker, older. She had given him some of her energy, that precious life she couldn't spare. He looked down at himself then and saw . . .

She had cast him in a suit of armor again, but it was not like the suit she had given him before, not the white knight's suit she had given him when he had invaded Kurodar's fortress. This was—well, it was a whole lot cooler, almost like something out of a Marvel Comics movie. The silver suit covered him like a second skin made out of metal. It clung to him so perfectly, so lightly, he could barely feel it was there. And yet it gleamed and shifted like Mariel gleamed and shifted. And he could somehow sense her strength all around him and the protection it gave him.

"It feels . . . weird," he said. "It feels like it's part of me."

"It is part of you. It's connected to your spirit. It *is* your spirit in a way, the outer manifestation of it. Your faith wasn't strong enough to carry it before, but it is now. I can feel it."

For another moment, Rick looked down at the silver suit with a kind of awe. Then he raised his eyes to her and nodded. "Yes," was all he said. "It is."

"You remember I taught you how to change the reality of the Realm with the power of your spirit . . ."

"Yeah, yeah, definitely," said Rick. With enough focus, he could change the shape of himself. He could flash from place to place like Favian . . .

"This armor will increase that power," she said. "It will respond to your thoughts and act swiftly. It won't make you invulnerable. Everyone is vulnerable to injury and death. But as long as your faith stays strong, it will give you more power than you ever knew you had."

Once more, as he looked up at her, at the majesty of her face, he yearned to tell her the whole truth about what was going to happen, about who she was, about how he couldn't rescue her from this place . . .

"Mariel . . ."

But again, she silenced him, raising a liquid hand. "Go. Quickly." It was always like this between them. He had never had a quiet moment to talk to her, to get to know her. "You have to reach the interface," she said.

Rick hesitated, but there was nothing he could say. "Where is it? How far? Is it in the Golden City?"

Mariel nodded, but she said, "It's in the City of the Dead." And then she added: "Follow the mist."

30. A TRAITOR'S
LEGACY

ALONE-ALL ALONE—in his office, Commander Mars watched the weapon on the screen. The Battle Station rolled against the backdrop of the stars, its energy panels turned toward the sun, its cannon turned toward earth. In a corner of the screen, the power meter filled slowly with green light. It was already nearly half full.

Mars sat in his high-backed leather swivel chair, surrounded by his shelves of books, his Persian rug, the pictures on his wall. His underground room had been made up to look like a study in a comfortable home somewhere.

And Mars looked like a man in his study, thinking. He sat with one elbow propped on the chair arm, his right hand held up to his face. His chin was propped on his thumb, his index finger raised alongside his forehead. He gazed at the animation on the screen and a small, joyless smile played at one corner of his mouth.

Like a video game, he was thinking. *The whole thing is like one big video game.*

It really did seem like that, down here, far away from

people, far away from the cities and farms and forests and fields that would burn to cinders if that weapon went off. A video game . . . The Battle Station on the screen . . . the boy, Dial, in the Realm . . . the Boars and Harpies and gigantic Cobras that had invaded the MindWar compound, nearly destroying his guard . . . It was all like a video game, as if they were all living inside the mad imagination of a teenager with a controller.

It was madness. Madness. But it was nowhere near as mad as what had happened to him. Nothing could be any crazier than that.

Mars's shoulders lifted and fell on a sigh. His belly felt hollow—not as if he were hungry, but as if his insides had been scooped out with a spoon, leaving him soulless, empty. He had not always felt like that. Once he had felt he had a solid core, a core of honor, of patriotism, of commitment and courage. Now all that was gone. How had it happened? How had he become a traitor?

Step-by-step, he thought.

It was true. He really had been a patriot once. He really had had a sense of honor. He had served his country in the Navy, in the intelligence service, and here, in the MindWar Project. He had always put the nation first, the mission first. Everything in his life came second to the job that had to be done. How had he gone from being that man to being what he was?

He'd been blackmailed, he told himself. He'd been tricked. He'd succumbed to fear . . .

That's what he told himself. But one word kept coming into his mind, ringing in his mind like a persistent bell.

Pride.

Pride goes before destruction, and a haughty spirit before a fall.

Wasn't that what the Bible said? He would have to ask the Traveler, Mars thought with self-lacerating irony. The Traveler knew his Bible, that was for sure. Mars hadn't read it since he was a boy.

But yes, he knew about pride, all right. He knew it was pride that had gotten him here. He had set out to protect the people of his country from foreign invaders, but soon he had found he was protecting them from themselves, from what he thought were their own foolish ideas. Without realizing it, he had come to feel superior to the very public he served. He had come to feel he was strong and wise and they were weak and stupid and needed him to watch over them. Soon, he wasn't serving his country at all anymore. Not really. He was serving his sense of himself, his sense of his own mighty strength and superiority. And that sense of superiority grew until he thought no one could question him, no one could second-guess him. He was so sure of himself, he didn't need to discuss his plans with colleagues or consult with his superiors or get permission from the elected officials in government who were his bosses or from anyone at all. That was why, when he conceived his idea to trap Moros and Axis, it had been easy for Moros to turn the trap around and spring it on him. They had smelled his pride like dogs smell food and they had come rushing to devour him.

And now, by his own fault, the country he had sworn to protect, the country he still loved, was about to be hit by a weapon more powerful than any ever known to man.

Unless a teenage boy could stop it by playing a deadly video game better than his opponents.

Madness.

The green light in the power meter at the bottom of the screen rose another notch. Mars swallowed something bitter.

There was a light tap at the door.

"Come in," he muttered.

The door to his office opened and Miss Ferris stepped in.

Mars swiveled slightly in his chair so he could see her. He could also see the guards who were standing in the hall—who had been standing in the hall for an hour now, making sure he did not escape. "I thought you were with the others."

"I was," she said. "I was monitoring Rick in the portal room."

He nodded. "But you left to find me. It must be something important."

There was a pause as Miss Ferris stood there in the doorway looking at him.

"I wanted to tell you they're here," she said. Her voice, as usual, held no emotion.

But Mars knew whom she meant: the officers had arrived to arrest him. They would take him into custody. After that, a public trial, disgrace, prison . . . maybe even execution. He would deserve execution if Kurodar managed to get the Battle Station charged up. Millions would die. Whole states would be in flames. And it would all be his fault . . . He would deserve whatever punishment they gave him.

"Do you want me to tell them to come for you or . . . ?" Miss Ferris's voice trailed off, leaving the sentence half finished.

Mars quietly shook his head. "I'll come up."

He swiveled around and stood. He took one final glance around his comfortable room. He would not have such comfortable quarters again, not ever. He would never have his freedom again.

Finally, he turned to look down at Miss Ferris. She met his gaze steadily, her face expressionless. As usual.

"How's it going in there?" he asked her.

"It worked," she said. "Rick is in the Golden City. If he can reach the interface . . . we have a chance."

He nodded. "Well . . . I hope they succeed."

"We all hope so," she said—very coldly. As usual.

Mars straightened his stance, trying to ready himself for what was coming. There was nothing else to say. It was time for him to go upstairs and turn himself in.

He walked to the door. Miss Ferris's eyes followed him closely as he moved. She never looked away. Her gaze was so intense, he finally stopped right at the threshold of the room and faced her. He knew what she was thinking. Of course he did. But he asked her anyway, "What is it, Miss Ferris? Is there something you want?"

There was a moment of silence as Miss Ferris continued to stare at him blankly. Then, in that same robotic voice, she said, "I sent a young Marine to his death in the Realm on your orders."

He nodded. He felt sorry for her. He knew how much she had felt that mistake, despite the way she locked up her emotions. "Try not to blame yourself," he said quietly. "The mission was right. The mistake was mine."

"But it was you I was following. I was ready to do whatever you said. I . . . I worshipped the ground you walked on."

He turned away. He could no longer meet her eyes. "I worshipped the ground I walked on too," he said. "I guess we both made the same mistake."

He stepped out of the room.

"But if I don't follow my commanding officer . . . ," Miss Ferris said behind him, and a note almost of desperation entered her voice. "If I don't follow my superior, who can I follow?"

Mars didn't answer. He didn't know the answer. He couldn't help her. He couldn't even help himself.

Two soldiers with automatic rifles were waiting for him in the hall. They moved to stand on either side of him.

Then the three of them marched off together, leaving Miss Ferris standing alone.

31. MYST

FOLLOW THE MIST.

That was what Mariel had told him—then the shape of her had dissolved before his eyes and spilled down into the basin, scattering into dribs and droplets, disappearing in between the crockery to flow away, out of sight. Rick did not know when he would see her again . . . if he would see her again . . . if he would live to see her again . . .

He looked at Favian. Favian floated beside him, shimmering, his mouth open, his eyes wide. He looked almost paralyzed with fear. Rick tried to give him a smile of encouragement, but the best he could do was to tilt his head toward the dining hall's far door.

"Guess we better get to it," he said.

He moved to the door, his footsteps heavy on the dining hall floor. The silver armor that coated his body flowed with him. Physically he could feel it only as a sort of thin rippling presence around him. But he felt the power of it, the strength. He wondered what cool things he could get the armor to do.

Favian flashed after him. His feet never touched the

floor and so his movement didn't make a sound. Rick reached the door and drew it open.

Follow the mist.

Rick looked out and understood.

Rick and Favian stood side by side, looking up a long corridor. It rose steadily out of shadow into light. At the top of the rising hall there was an open doorway. After being in the dark so long, Rick found the yellow light washing in through the doorway almost blinding. It made him squint.

Just at the place where the light spilled into the hall, Rick could detect the first drifting tendrils of mist.

"I guess that's the mist we're supposed to follow," he said to Favian.

"I guess," Favian said weakly. "Kind of spooky-looking."

Rick didn't answer. He began moving up the passageway. After a moment, Favian flickered at his side.

As the light of the doorway grew closer, Rick felt himself getting tighter inside, more nervous. What was this monster Mariel had seen guarding the interface? Could he fight it? Could he win?

Baba Yaga's words haunted him: *You must go into the belly of the beast. You must face the horror he cannot face.*

He still didn't know exactly what those words meant. Something about those horrific images he had seen in the witch's table. But what? He felt he was going to find out, and soon.

He and Favian reached the end of the corridor. They hesitated at the threshold of the doorway. The mist blew in and curled and rose around their feet. Rick looked at the anxious Favian and Favian anxiously looked at Rick.

"Well, buddy, I guess this is it," Rick said. "This will decide it one way or the other."

Favian nodded very slightly, very slowly. "I guess." He peered at Rick anxiously. "And your dad will really build me a portal out of here?" he said.

Rick nodded. "That's what he told me."

"And you trust him, right? I mean, he's not the kind of guy who would lie or anything, is he?"

"No, he's not," said Rick with certainty—certainty he hadn't felt for quite some time. "He's a good man, a man you can trust." He felt a surge of warmth as he said it. He was lucky, he thought, to have a father he could say that about.

Favian nodded. "Okay. Okay. Okay," he repeated nervously.

Rick forced himself to smile. "Come on, you blue dipstick," he said. "Let's go fight the bad guys."

And they stepped through the door.

32. CITY OF FOG

MOLLY STOOD OVER Rick's sleeping body, holding his hand. Miss Ferris had returned to the makeshift portal room and was standing beside her, her expression blank, her eyes gazing at nothing. On the monitors on the wall, the Battle Station turned in space. Its power meter, Molly saw, was now more than halfway full. Ninety minutes left, she thought. If that.

"Traveler?" said the techie Chuck.

Lawrence Dial and Professor Jameson sat side by side, working their keyboards relentlessly. At Chuck's call, Dial blinked through the code reflected on the lenses of his glasses. As if he had been wakened from a dream, he turned hazily to the tech. Molly could see his mind was still distracted.

"What is it?" he said.

"I don't know," said Chuck. "Look at this."

The Traveler looked at Chuck's screen, and Molly looked too. The view of the Realm had changed. There were simple, pixilated images of streets and buildings, but it was all unfocused, unclear. A shifting patch of blackness was moving over the image, obscuring different sections at different times.

And where were the figures of Rick and Favian? Where had they gone?

"What's happening?" she heard herself say . . . but neither Chuck nor the Traveler answered her. They were bending their heads together as they stared at the screen. "What is that on the screen, that black patch?"

The Traveler shook his head. "I don't know what it is."

"Me either," said Chuck. "And look here."

Using the computer mouse, he moved the image. There was an even darker black patch moving off to one side.

"It doesn't look like a program exactly," he said.

"No," said the Traveler. "It's almost like an organic structure. It seems to be generating the mist that's blocking the image elsewhere."

"Yes," said Chuck. "The mist seems to emanate from there."

"He's protecting the interface," the Traveler murmured. "And anything he might have hiding in there."

Molly couldn't stand the way they were talking, as if it were all some kind of interesting experiment, as if Rick's life were not in danger.

"Where's Rick?" she said. "Why can't I see his figure anymore? Where is he?"

The Traveler looked at her over his shoulder as if he'd forgotten she was there. "Don't worry," he told her.

"Why not?"

The Traveler blinked. "Well, because it won't help, for one thing." He turned back to look at the screen. "Rick is heading into this mist. Whatever's there, he's going to have to face it." He glanced at her again. "That's what he went in for, Molly. That's what we sent him to do."

Molly stared at him, amazed. "You sound so calm about it! He's your son."

The Traveler gave her a small smile. "Actually, I already know who he is."

"Yes, but . . . ," Molly started to say. But what *could* she say? The Traveler was right. This was what they had sent Rick into the Realm to do. She hated that they sounded so calm about it all. But what good would it do to sound excited or panicked?

"We're just going to have to wait and see what—" the Traveler began to tell her.

But before he could finish, Molly's father, Professor Jameson, let out a gasp. He leaned away from his own monitor and his big body went back against his swivel chair. It was as if something on the screen had struck him. He continued staring at the numbers on the screen in front of him.

"Dad? What's the matter? What's happening?" Molly asked him.

The Traveler rolled his chair up behind Jameson so he could look past his shoulder at his computer.

"Look at that!" Professor Jameson said to him. "I . . . I can't believe it!"

The Traveler could only look on in shocked silence.

———

The streets of the Golden City were empty. Even the dead were gone. Rick and Favian moved slowly along the pavement through the ever-thickening mist. Rick gleamed in his silver armor. Favian flashed a shimmering blue.

Rick's eyes kept moving as he looked all around him. *Weird place, this Golden City,* he kept thinking. It didn't seem real and yet it didn't seem totally a dream either. It wasn't like some fairy kingdom in a video game exactly. It was more like something you half remembered. A place you'd been to that you couldn't quite recall. It was meant to be beautiful, Rick could see that. And parts of it were beautiful. There were buildings that looked like some sort of great cake, with towers and onion-shaped domes and golden facades lit by sourceless rays of light. There were great open squares with towers and statues that seemed to stretch almost to the edge of the horizon. There were wonderful bridges flanked with lacy stone balustrades and presided over by statues of winged lions. And yet as beautiful as these places were, they—and everything here—looked solemn and sad, spiritless and hollow. Empty shells under a yellow sky that had darkened to a color like amber as the day wore on.

The streets were empty everywhere. It looked to Rick as if there had been a catastrophe and everyone had been evacuated or killed. This also struck him as sad. In fact, the whole place just seemed to pulse with melancholy.

Rick stopped, feeling the heaviness of the atmosphere inside him. Favian stopped, too, hovering in the air.

"It's like a ghost town," Rick said.

"I know," said Favian. "I hate it here. I've been stuck here I don't know how long. But there's nowhere else to go. All the rest of the Realm is blackness. We thought it was bad before when we had the Blue Wood and the Scarlet Plain to wander through. But now . . . stuck here . . . dying slowly . . . I sure hope your dad can make that portal."

"He will, don't worry," Rick murmured, but he was barely paying attention to Favian's anxieties. He was trying to figure out which way to go.

They had come to a crossroads. Up ahead was a long street of ornate concrete buildings lit by enchanting green and golden lights. It went on a long way and seemed to narrow in the distance to a vanishing point. To his left was a canal, a passageway flooded with silver water. Small boats lined the quays under more buildings with pastel colors. To his right, a wide-open square with a huge building in the center of it: another one of those fancy buildings with onion domes of various shapes and colors.

The mist blew around Rick's and Favian's legs as they turned in one direction and the next, trying to make up their minds. It dissipated and thinned over the square, and stayed about the same on the street of buildings. To Rick, it seemed to grow thicker over the mercurial water of the canal.

"This way then," he said.

253

He headed off, and Favian followed.

They moved along the canal on a rolling sidewalk bordered by a low stone balustrade. With every step they took, the mist seemed to grow thicker before them, the buildings and colored lights growing dim and distant. A chill crept over Rick. He could feel it even with the silver armor coating his skin.

Even Favian, creature of light that he was, felt it. "It's chilly, huh."

"Yeah. The whole place feels kind of chilly and sad."

"And spooky."

"Yeah, and spooky."

"You're almost there."

Another voice. Both Rick and Favian looked around, startled.

"Don't stop now."

It was Mariel. Her words echoed all around them through the empty air.

"The water!" said Favian.

That was it. Rick looked toward the canal. He moved closer to the balustrade and peered over into the silver flow. The darkening amber sky was reflected and refracted on the moving metallic surface. Half a dozen colors seemed to shift and blend and separate in the depths of the current.

But she was there. Mariel. Rick could see her: a sort of suggestion of a shape moving with the movement of the water.

"Look to where the mist thickens up ahead," her voice said to him, speaking it seemed from all around him. *"Be ready, Rick."*

He nodded. "I'm ready," he said. Which was sort of a lie. He wasn't ready at all. How could he be ready? He didn't even know what he was going to face. But really, it didn't matter whether he was ready or not. He wasn't turning back for anything. So in that sense, anyway, he was ready enough.

Rick and Favian continued to walk along the canal. They could feel Mariel flowing along in the canal to their left.

"It's good to have you here," Rick said to her. It was. He felt stronger, safer, with Mariel nearby.

"I can only go with you as far as the graveyard," Mariel said, "not beyond. The fog cloud blocks the flow of water—and light. There's a stream that goes around the graveyard and gets closer to the interface, but I'm running out of strength . . ."

Rick didn't answer. He could hear the weakness in Mariel's voice. She was beginning to sound old.

As if to give her some encouragement, Favian piped up, "Rick's dad is going to make portals to get us out of here!"

Rick didn't say anything. And for a moment, Mariel didn't say anything either.

But then she did. She said, "Is that true, Rick?"

Before he could answer, Favian broke in like an excited

child. "Yeah, if anyone can do it, Rick's dad can. He's like a genius or something. Right, Rick?"

Rick walked alongside the canal in silence. The mist twisted and roiled and grew thicker around him. He could feel his friends waiting for his answer.

"Mariel," he said, "what do you remember? What do you remember about before you came here? About RL?"

In the silence that followed, he shivered at the cold. The silver armor rippled on his flesh, almost as if it were imitating the rippling movement of Mariel in the water, as if she were as close to him as his own skin.

"I can't remember very much at all," Mariel said then. "Hardly anything. Sometimes, when I close my eyes, I can hear people laughing—laughing and talking like friends. I must have had friends, I guess. And I know the grass is not supposed to be red, but green. And the sky should be blue not yellow. I don't know why I know those things, but I do. It must be something I remember. And I think . . . ," she began and then her voice seemed to sink back into the mist.

"What?" said Rick.

"I think someone must have loved me," said Mariel. "A man. There are times, when it's very quiet, when I'm all alone . . . there are times when I can feel his lips against my lips . . ."

Rick listened to her intently. He was wondering: How could she know these things? How could she remember anything, if she was just a program, just a code? They must have been some other person's memories, or fragments of many people's memories, held within the connectome generated by the black box.

There was a sound of distant thunder, a soft, ominous rumble very far away. Mariel's voice broke off.

"Here we are," she said then.

Rick stopped and looked around him. The mist had grown very thick while he was listening to her. It was almost a fog now. It shifted and parted and came together on every side of him. Peering through it, Rick saw an opening off to his right. Down a narrow lane, there was an iron gate. Beyond the iron gate, there was a field. As the mist shifted, Rick saw statues and stones and small towers and a large building beyond them. It was a graveyard, almost hidden in the dense and shifting mist.

The sight of the cemetery chilled him, but it was what he saw beyond the graves that made him quail.

It was off in the middle distance, not that far. It was like nothing he'd ever seen before, nothing in Real Life, anyway. Beyond the graveyard, the sky seemed to just . . . go out. Like a candle flame when you blow on it. Like a lightbulb when you throw the switch. The whole world beyond the graveyard seemed to just . . . go out. And in its place, there was a wall of burgeoning, shifting, solid cloud boiling and churning like some great wizard's potion. Now and then, light flashed from inside the heart of the miasma: lightning. And in the moment after came that low grumble of thunder.

"What . . . what's that?" said Favian. His voice trembled.

"Guess that's the fog cloud Mariel was talking about," said Rick—and he could hear that his own voice wasn't all that steady either.

"You have to pass through the cloud to reach the interface," said Mariel. With every word she spoke, more of her strength and energy seemed to drain away.

Rick and Favian stood staring across the misty graveyard at that boiling wall of solid atmosphere. As the thunder subsided, another sound replaced it. A low, rhythmic boom. *Boom. Boom. Boom.* Very soft. Very far away. But all the same, Rick could feel the pavement quake underneath his feet every time the sound reached him. He felt himself shrink inside his armor, fear pulling him into himself.

It was the sound of footsteps. Something pacing back and forth. Something huge.

Rick's confidence left him all at once. It was like water dropping out of a bucket when the bottom gives way. Suddenly, he knew with absolute certainty: He was going to die in there. He was going to walk into that cloud and meet whatever was pacing inside it, waiting for him, and he was never going to come back. The best he could hope for was that God would let him destroy the interface before the monster overcame him. That he could stop the attack on his country—on RL—before he lost his life.

Taking a long and shuddering breath, he turned away from the spectacle of the lightning-laced wall of cloud. He turned back to the canal. He realized he had no choice anymore. He had to tell Mariel the truth. He couldn't walk into that cloud—he couldn't die—and leave her to believe that he would somehow save her. The truth might break her heart. It might make her hate him. But he had to tell her. He couldn't die with the lie on his head.

He moved close to the balustrade and looked over the stone rail into the silver water. He felt Favian at his shoulder, hovering nearby, curious.

"Mariel," he said.

And her voice surrounded him—and the warmth and strength of her presence was as close to him as the armor was close to his skin. "What is it, Rick?"

"There's something I have to tell you."

———

"What?" said Molly. "What is it?"

The Traveler and her father—and now Chuck the tech guy, too—were gathered around Professor Jameson's computer, staring at the code rolling down the screen. They were all staring openmouthed as if they were looking at . . . well, who knew what? Molly had no clue what they were seeing. It made her want to scream with frustration.

"What is it?" she said again. "Is it Rick? Is he all right? Is something wrong?"

In answer—if you could call it an answer—Rick's father and her father turned to look at each other silently.

ANDREW KLAVAN

Chuck the tech guy turned to look at her. But none of them spoke.

"Daddy!" Molly cried out finally. "Tell me what's happening!"

Professor Jameson cleared his throat as if he were about to give a lecture.

"We're trying to isolate the code variation that keeps damaged avatars stuck inside the Realm," he told her.

"Yeah, yeah, I get that," Molly said impatiently, though she had only the vaguest idea what it meant.

"To do that . . . ," her father continued slowly, glancing at her only every other word as if he found it difficult to meet her eyes. "To do that, we were going to compare the code for Mariel's connectome with the code for Fabian Child's avatar. That way we could find the similarities in damage. Do you understand?"

"Yes. No. Sort of. I don't know. Why?" said Molly. "What's it mean? Why is everyone so excited?"

"As I was studying Mariel's connectome, the patterns began to seem familiar to me," her father continued.

"Familiar? Those numbers? What—"

Professor Jameson cut his daughter off. "You remember how you and Rick helped us out by coming in and letting us borrow your brain waves for our experiments in brain-computer interfaces?"

"Uh, yeah, sure, you hooked up some wires to our heads and—" Molly stopped talking abruptly as some inkling of what her father might be telling her began to filter into her mind. "You mean . . . ?"

It was the Traveler who started speaking now. "When Mars acted on his own and sent these first MindWarriors into the Realm without my knowledge, he used our research to build the avatars for Fabian and for Sergeant Posner. To try and limit the risk, he sent in one warrior who wasn't human, who was just a connectome, a collection of downloaded code. He used our research materials to accomplish that. And he chose the most complete connectome we made, the one that was nearly human because we were so familiar with the subject we were downloading that we could fill in the gaps ourselves."

Molly turned from the Traveler's mild gaze and stared back at her father. The large, shambling Professor Jameson finally looked directly at her.

"He chose your connectome, Molly," he said. "He used the download of your mind to build a MindWarrior."

"My . . . ," was all Molly could say. Her mouth had turned as dry as ashes.

"He used the download of your mind to create Mariel," Professor Jameson told his daughter.

"You mean . . . You mean I'm Mariel?" she asked softly.

"No, no, no, of course not. You're not Mariel," her father said. "But to all intents and purposes, Mariel is you."

Half a world away, Kurodar felt his power nearing its very peak. The Battle Station was completely under his control and was steadily charging, almost ready to fire. He could feel the efforts of the people in the American government trying to hack their way into it, to wrest it away from him, but he flicked their efforts off like so many flies with the merest effort of his mind. They could not touch him.

Meanwhile, in the Realm, what was left of the Realm, the Golden City, he sensed his nemesis, Rick Dial, moving toward the interface. This made him glad. The boy had defeated him twice, but Kurodar was certain it would not, and could not, happen again. The King of the Dead, the last defender of his territory, was virtually indestructible. It was a thing from the very core of his own mind, automatically drawing on the power of his imagination so that any damage Dial managed to inflict on it would be almost immediately repaired. What's more, it could do more than attack. It could create on its own, so that as often as Dial launched himself against it, he would find himself facing a full complement of reinforcements, a legion of destruction.

Kurodar was going to unleash an attack of unimaginable scope on the United States and, at the same time, he was going to kill the Traveler's son.

He was, at this moment, everything he had always wanted to be.

He had been dreaming of this day forever. When he was a little boy, he remembered looking at his father in his sharp, crisp KGB uniform. He remembered thinking his dad was almost like a god, inspiring fear in everyone who saw him, wielding the power of life and death. There could be no one, he had thought, more powerful than his father was. And he had wanted to become like that himself. Even as his father laughed at him for his ugliness, or made fun of him for being a weak, puny intellectual, or struck him in his drunken rages, dealing out humiliating beatings in front of his mother and in front of strangers . . . Even then, Kurodar worshipped the man and wanted to inherit his god-like strength.

Now he had. The King of the Dead was the very image of that father he admired—but with this twist: he had the son's mind, the son's genius. In MindWar, Kurodar had become the man he always wanted to be. He had become his father. He had become that god.

It was the point and purpose of all his work. And now nothing and no one could stop him.

———

As Rick peered down into the silver water of the canal, Mariel's face and form appeared to him faintly. He wasn't sure whether she was really visible beneath the glinting current or if he simply imagined her there as she would be. But he could feel it was she—her spirit, her essence. He could feel it in the response of the armor she had given him, the metallic second skin that rippled and shone over his entire body.

He drew a breath and when he let it out, it carried the words he had been holding inside him all this time.

"Mariel," he said down into the water, "I can't take you with me."

Mariel's voice rose up to him and surrounded him, filling the mist that hung everywhere. "I know that, Rick. I'm not strong enough anymore to break through the cloud. You'll have to go and face this last security bot alone. You'll have to—"

"No," he said, "that isn't what I meant. I meant I can't take you out of here. I can't take you out of the Realm."

Mariel didn't answer. It was Favian, hovering just behind Rick, who said sharply, "What? What do you mean? That's crazy. You said you could. Why not?"

Rick swallowed. He could feel the seconds ticking away, the Battle Station in RL charging, time running out. But he had to say this. He had to. "Mariel, you've done everything for me. I would never have survived this long without you. My sword, my armor, the fact that I can use my spirit to control the fabric of the Realm—you gave me all that and I'd've been dead a thousand times over if I didn't have it."

"That's right!" said Favian. "You'd've been killed if it weren't for her. We both would've been killed."

But Mariel remained silent.

"But see," Rick stumbled on, "Favian here, he's an avatar, like me. He's made out of the link between a living human being and a computer. I have to bring him back to free that human being from his interface with the Realm. So he can live, see. So he can go back to his life."

"But what about Mariel? What about her life?" Favian said. "She's got to live too."

Still Mariel said nothing.

"You, Mariel, you're not what Favian is," Rick said. "You're what's called a connectome. A computer-generated code that imitates a human mind." It was hard, but Rick finally forced it out. "Look, I'm not a science guy. I'm just a football player. But the bottom line is this: You're not a person, Mariel. You're a program. There's no you in RL. There never was. There's just a machine, generating code."

"That's crazy!" Favian cried out. "That's ridiculous! That's—"

Now Mariel finally spoke, cutting him off. "Rick, are you sure?" she said. And the sound of her voice made Favian stop talking. The sound of her voice made Rick stand straight, gripping the stone of the balustrade. He had never heard her sound this way before. He had never heard this tone of doubt and fear from her. But he heard them now. "I can't . . . ," she began. "I mean . . . it doesn't seem . . . I remember things . . . the laughter . . . the blue of the sky . . . I remember . . . that kiss . . . How is it possible if I'm just . . . ?"

Rick shook his head. "I don't know. I guess those are memories from the people they used to make your code. But I've seen what you are in RL, Mariel. You're a black box. Numbers on a screen."

It made Rick's heart ache to say it. And it made him ache even worse to hear the pleading tone that entered the voice of the woman who had been his source of strength and wisdom here. "But I feel . . . I feel so real . . . I remember things . . . I am someone. I know I am. I can't just be . . . a code. I'm a person. I'm real."

Rick shook his head. "You're real here. You're someone here. You are. But not in RL. I can't take you back to RL because there is no RL you. There's no person for you to become there. What you are here . . . It's everything you are. There's nothing else. I'm sorry, Mariel."

Mariel was silent. Rick could feel her anguish in the armor encasing him. It was awful. He could feel the very struggle of her mind to come to grips with the truth he was telling her. The moment of silence between them seemed to last forever.

Then she said in a steadier voice, "You're sure of this, Rick."

He nodded. "Yeah. I saw the box with my own eyes. Believe me, Mariel, if there were any way . . ."

"No, no, wait, this is crazy!" Favian shouted suddenly.

Rick glanced at him. The blue sprite flashed back and forth from one side of him to the other. "This is nuts! Of course she's a person! She's Mariel! We know her! We know who she is! There's gotta be some mistake."

Rick spoke through the tightness in his throat. "There's no mistake."

"There is!"

"I'm telling you, pal . . ."

But Favian's hand flashed out at him. "Don't you call me that. You're not my pal. You're not anyone's pal. You just came in here and used us, and now you're going to leave us behind here to die in this place."

"Not you . . ."

"You think I'd leave without Mariel? You think I'd desert my best friend?"

"There's no choice," said Rick. "You know I'd take her with me if I could. I care about her, man! Same as you. More than that. I . . ."

But his voice trailed off. His emotions were too confused to put into words. He loved Molly, he knew he did. Now that he had seen the truth of it, there was no unseeing it. She lived and breathed and he wanted to be with her forever, was meant to be with her forever. As for the feelings he had for Mariel, this silver phantom who had guided him through the terrors of this place . . . well, what could he make of them? She wasn't real. She wasn't a person. His attachment to her was as fantastic as this entire world.

"You don't care about anything except your mission," Favian said. He wasn't yelling anymore. His voice had dropped to a dangerous undertone. "You used us for what you could get out of us and now you're going to leave us here to suffocate inside this nightmare . . ."

"*Favian!*"

With that word, Mariel erupted out of the canal water. With a silver splash, she rose above them, majestic and commanding. As the metallic water took her shape, Rick saw again that face and form that touched the deepest parts of him. He saw the rapid aging that was sucking the life out of her, and he saw the sorrow—the deep sorrow—in her expression, but none of it changed the strength and compassion that were always in her eyes. Her voice filled the mist, strong again and steady, but Rick could feel the depth of her grief in the armor clinging to his skin. She was going to die here—and she had never even lived. She had never seen the green grass she remembered or the blue sky, and she would never see them now.

"Rick is only telling us what he knows," she said to Favian. "He can't change it. If he could, he would. You can't hate a man for speaking the truth. In the end, the truth is all we have."

Rick looked at Favian—at his face made of shifting particles of light. He saw the fury of betrayal in the sprite's eyes. He knew there was nothing he could say.

"Your time is running short," said Mariel to Rick, forcing her feelings down completely, all business now. "You have to get to the interface. You have to shut this place down before Kurodar destroys RL."

"What do I care what happens in RL?" said Favian. "I'm never going back there anyway."

"You are," said Mariel. "You're not what I am . . ."

"Why? Because he said so? Why should we trust him? He didn't even tell us about this until he had to."

"Favian . . . ," Rick said, but that's all he said. His friend was talking crazy, he knew that. But there was no argument you could make to a guy who was determined not to believe the truth. He turned away from the blue man and raised his eyes to the liquid silver form above him. "I better go," he told her. And then he said, "Mariel . . . ," but he didn't know what else to tell her.

She gave him a queenly nod. "I understand, Rick," she said. "It's all right."

"I'm sorry."

"I know."

He took a step back from the balustrade. He glanced at Favian again. "You coming, man, or what?"

"No," said Favian, giving him a stony stare.

"Favian," Mariel said. She lifted a flowing hand and pointed toward the graveyard. "Go."

"No," said Favian. "I won't. Not with him. This is wrong. This is insane."

For another second, Rick looked at him. Then he raised his eyes one last time to Mariel.

She met his gaze and he felt her spirit not just in his armor but in his heart. He did not know how to leave her behind. She was special. Unique. She had . . . What could he call it? A unique generosity of spirit, a power of outward-flowing kindness he had never felt before. He had never known anyone like her and he doubted he ever would again.

She nodded at him. He nodded back. Then he forced himself to turn away.

He forced himself to turn toward the graveyard, the stones and statues covered with drifting mist. He looked beyond it to the churning, boiling wall of cloud with the lightning flashing in it and the thunder rumbling and those gigantic pacing footsteps within making the whole Realm shiver.

Boom. Boom. Boom.

He hated to leave his friends like this. He felt absolutely sure he was going to die in that cloud, and the idea that they would remember him as the would-be hero who had failed them, the man who betrayed them—it was tough to bear.

He glanced at Favian and got the stony stare again.

He turned back to the roiling cloud.

"All right then," he said softly. "Alone."

And he started to walk toward the lightning.

33. MORTAL COMBAT

THE WHITE FIGURE that represented Rick moved in and out of view on Chuck's misty monitor as it traveled toward that great central black stain that swallowed all the other images of the Realm.

Holding Rick's hand, Molly watched the picture on the screen and thought, *Mariel is you.*

At first the words her father spoke had overwhelmed her. She could not make sense of them. She could not take them in. But as the moments passed and as their meaning filtered into her understanding, a strange, warm sense of gladness went over her.

The black box went on blinking in its coffin, faceless, soulless, nameless, and yet Molly felt the presence of the imaginary woman inside it, the woman who had protected Rick and inspired him and fought beside him.

Mariel. Mariel was her. Mariel's mind was made from her mind. Mariel was just an image of her brain.

And yes, it made her glad. It wasn't just that Rick—in admiring Mariel, in depending on Mariel, in, let's face it, loving Mariel—had been admiring and depending on and loving the essence of herself all along . . . Oh well, it *was* that. Yes, it was. Sure it was. But it was more too. Or at least, she thought, maybe it could be more.

The white figure on Chuck's screen reached the edge of the darkness. The silver figure of Mariel and the blue figure of Favian had vanished behind him. Rick was about to walk into that unknown blackness all alone.

"Daddy," she said—speaking aloud even before she was sure of what she was going to say.

Her father stopped tapping at his keyboard and turned to her.

"Professor Dial," she said.

And the Traveler turned too.

Both men looked at her.

"Connect me to her," Molly said.

Neither Dial nor her father answered. They both simply gazed at her, the Traveler blinking behind his glasses.

"Connect me to the box," she said. She gestured at the glass coffin that held Mariel's machine. "There are, you know, what do you call it, outlets, plugs in the box. You can put wires in there. Connect my brain to Mariel's code. So I can go into the Realm too. So I can be with Rick. So I can help him. So he doesn't have to go into the darkness alone."

Now Chuck was looking at her, too, and Molly could even feel Miss Ferris's eyes on her. The silence seemed to continue for hours.

Then Professor Jameson said, "But . . ."

Then there was more silence.

Then Chuck said, "But we can't do that."

Then there was even more silence.

Then the Traveler said softly, "Actually . . . we probably could."

———

Rick moved toward the graveyard. It was a journey from sorrow to fear. Behind him was Mariel, mourning, and also Favian, enraged. He hated to leave them that way, and the thought of it sat in his mind with a dark weight of sadness. Ahead of him loomed the misty graveyard and the flashing, churning wall of cloud. With every step he took, he felt the fear of it growing inside him.

But he did not look back. He kept his eyes on the stormy miasma. He had no choice but to go forward . . . No, that wasn't true. He did have a choice. There was always a choice. But there was only one right choice, and that was the choice he was making. On he went.

He reached the wrought-iron gate of the graveyard. The mist rose up and swirled around him, chilling him through the thin silver armor. He reached out and felt the gate's cold iron and pushed it open. It creaked like a ghost house door.

Rick walked steadily into the cemetery. The mist closed around him, and in the mist he caught glimpses of figures that seemed to watch him as he moved among the graves. They were stone statues: of mourning angels, of women shrouded in cowls, of sorrowful cherubs perched on head-stones, and of bearded men peering grim and serious from the far side of death. The mist made these figures seem dim and ghostly. They formed out of nothing, became solid, began to fade, then were gone.

Rick shivered. It was cold here, and a wind was blow-ing, a swirling chill air that made the tendrils of fog spiral and blend and break apart again. Litter and dust blew and tumbled around his feet. An old yellow page from a magazine wafted by right beneath him, and Rick caught a glimpse of a picture on it, a picture of a building in a for-eign land. He recognized the building right away: it was that first church he had entered when he came here, the place where he had first glimpsed the Realm's deep black-ness inside the coffin, where he and Favian had fought their way to the spiral stairs and the chamber of Baba Yaga.

He glanced up as the wall of cloud before him flashed and rumbled. When he looked down again, the magazine page had blown away. His eyes lifted and scanned the mist all around him nervously. All those gravestones and tombs standing motionless—it was creepy. It looked like a scene in a movie just before some phantom or zombie rises up to attack . . . Well, it could happen, couldn't it? Why not? This was the MindWar Realm after all. He'd seen weirder stuff than that here.

That's why he started and caught his breath when he spotted a motion at the corner of his eye. His hand mov-ing to the hilt of his sword, he looked toward the motion.

Something lying against a headstone . . . Cautiously, he moved closer.

It was just a book, a child's picture book blown up close to the stone. The chill wind was making the pages flutter. As Rick watched, the wind dropped, and the book lay open. There was an illustration on the open page that Rick recognized immediately. It was a picture of a green viny monster rising out of a swamp. As the breeze rose again and the page trembled, Rick had time to read a few words beneath the drawing:

Bagiennik—a water demon who lives in the . . .

Then the wind blew and the pages began fluttering by again.

Rick understood. All this litter around him—it was the detritus of Kurodar's mind. All these graves—they were his dead memories. This was the part of the terrorist's mind that held thoughts he barely knew he had. Images that had been living inside him since he was a child. It was a strange idea. The whole Golden City was constructed of these things—these things Kurodar had seen in his youth and only half remembered. The Russian church, the city streets, the canal . . . and the demon from the child's picture book that had probably once given him nightmares.

Rick was about to leave the book behind and start walking toward the cloud again when softly, nearly buried within the growing whisper of the breeze, an eerie sound came to him: the sound of high, cackling laughter.

Rick's mouth went dry. He licked his lips. He looked around the graveyard.

But when the cackle came again, he realized that no, it wasn't coming from the graveyard, it was coming from the headstone beneath him, from the book.

Sure enough, as he looked down, the pages of the book against the headstone blew again and came to a stop, and he saw the drawing of the witch on the page, and the name:

Baba Yaga.

The drawing showed a hideous crone—even more hideous than the witch had been in person. She was stirring some gooey mixture in a big pot. The mixture was bloodred, and there were weird bits and pieces of who knows what in it.

And as Rick gazed down at the picture, the witch in the drawing looked up at him!

He gasped aloud. The drawing had come to life! The picture of Baba Yaga grinned at him, toothless. She laughed that high, cackling laugh again.

"Don't forget, Rick," she said, cackling. "You hold the truth inside you. The truth is your greatest weapon."

The wind rose even higher, and the book came free of its place against the stone and tumbled away into the mist, gone.

Rick shook his head to clear away the image of the talking picture. Had it been real? Who could say? Was anything real in this place?

He started moving again, through the mist, among the graves.

He came nearer to the wall of cloud. It loomed above him, more fearsome with every step he took. Now Rick had to crane his neck to look up to the top of it. But there was no top. The cloud wall blotted out everything above him, as high as the sky and higher. It stood as far to the left and right as Rick could see. The cloud was dark and full and ominous like storm clouds just before they break. It was moving with a thick, bubbling motion like boiling tar, and the sound of it was a steady, hoarse roar. Now and then, the lightning flashed inside it. It seemed to turn the cloud translucent so that Rick caught glimpses of the thing on the other side: a silhouette of a hulking creature the size of a building. In the split second it was visible, the dark shadow moved behind the cloud, and its footsteps shook the earth. *Boom. Boom. Boom.* Then the lightning faded and the steps were drowned out by rolling thunder.

Rick reached the cloud. He stopped. He stood before the boiling wall, staring into the darkness of it. Without the lightning, that darkness was impenetrable. He breathed in deeply, trying to work up the courage to step into the storm, but for another long moment he hesitated. He could feel the miasmic dampness of the cloud on his skin. He could feel it right through his armor, a damp that was clammy and slick with filth. He hated the thought of entering.

His silver armor rippled on his skin.

As long as your faith stays strong, it will give you more power than you ever knew you had.

Rick prayed for courage. On the instant—almost as he

thought the words—the prayer was answered, and more. Courage was all he asked for, and it would have been enough, but not only did the courage come to him but also some living sense of love that he knew would sustain him even if things came to the worst. His father was in that love, his mother, his goofy brother, Raider, Molly too; the love contained them all and they were all with him and the love was with him and he was no longer afraid.

Rick stepped into the storm cloud.

———

"The code in the black box is the code we got from your mind," the Traveler told Molly. "In theory, you should be able to join your thoughts to that code seamlessly."

The techs had brought in another cot for her. She was lying down on it now, right beside Rick. Dial had put a headband on her with wires that would plug into the black box. She could feel her heart fluttering with fear, but she didn't care. Fear was only fear. It would not stop her.

"What that connection will be like or whether it will give you any power over Mariel, I don't know. But you might be able to give her some of your strength."

Standing right behind him, and towering over him, Professor Jameson licked his lips with anxiety. "What if Mariel gives her some of her weakness?"

Molly tried to smile at him. "Don't worry, Daddy," she said.

He smiled back. "Why not?"

"Because it doesn't help."

The Traveler glanced over his shoulder at Chuck.

"We lost him," said Chuck. "He's in that fogbank. I can't track him anymore."

The Traveler looked down at Molly again. "If we're going to do this . . ."

Molly nodded. "Do it," she said.

Lawrence Dial took a deep breath and plugged Molly into the black box.

Molly never lost her RL consciousness. She never fully entered the Realm. Instead, she went into a kind of fugue state where it seemed her dreams and the world blended together. On the one hand, she was aware of the make-shift portal room around her: the techs, the monitors, the glass coffins, Rick on his cot, her father and Professor Dial gazing down at her with a mixture of worry and scientific curiosity. On the other hand, an image had formed in her mind. Like a daydream, only much, much clearer. It was an image of a city in mist. A field in the distance . . . a field of stones . . . a graveyard, that's what it was! And there was a man there. Or not a man, but a fairy or sprite, made of blue light. Favian, yes. And as she looked out at those images, she had a sense of herself, her own body, changing form, becoming less solid, more liquid, a flow of energy with fluid, changing outlines. More than that, there were new thoughts coming to her. There was new knowledge. They were not her thoughts. It was not her knowledge. But somehow she knew what she hadn't known before.

She focused her mind as hard as she could. She tried to think into the things she saw, the things she felt, the things she knew.

She thought, *We have to go with Rick. We have to help Rick. We have to.*

"We have to go with Rick," said Mariel.

Favian looked up, startled by the sound of her voice. Suddenly she sounded stronger, surer. Suddenly her figure had become younger, more powerful. Her voice filled the mist around him.

"We have to help him," she said.

"Why should we?" Favian spat out bitterly. "He doesn't care about us. He was going to leave you here—leave you to die . . ." His voice trailed off. He was still angry at what Rick had said, but already the anger was beginning to curdle in him and turn to guilt. He had lost his temper, and in his rage, he had let his friend walk into danger alone. He knew it was wrong. Even as he was doing it, he knew. But the anger was like another person inside him, a person telling him to do what he knew he shouldn't. He'd obeyed the anger and now he wished he hadn't.

"Favian," said Mariel. "Listen to me. I can't explain it all to you now. But Rick will not leave me. Rick loves me and I love him, and we are going to be together."

"But he just said—" Favian began.

Mariel cut him off. "It doesn't matter what he said. He doesn't know what I know. Trust me, Favian. It's going to be all right. But we have to go to him. We have to help him. He'll die alone if we don't."

Favian didn't need that much encouragement. He was sorry for what he'd done. He nodded.

"All right."

Mariel turned and gazed off into the distance as if she were thinking. "There is . . . there is a stream . . . that goes around the graveyard . . . ," she said haltingly.

"Yes, you said," said Favian. "But you said you were too weak . . ."

"I'm not too weak. Not anymore. You hurry after Rick through the graveyard. I will meet you on the other side if I can."

Favian hesitated only one more second. "And he won't leave you here. You'll come out with us."

"I promise Rick and I will be together," she told him. "If we live through this."

Rick stepped into the cloud and his first thought was *Yuh-uck!*

It was disgusting here. It was beyond disgusting. It was hyperdisgusting. It was, like, electric disgusting amped to blast the back of your head off with disgust. That's how disgusting it was.

The inside of the cloud seemed to be made of some sort of sewage soup: a thick, greasy goulash with chunks of pure nasty floating past. The stench was indescribable—and if you could have described it, it would have been unbelievable. It curled up Rick's nose and down to the back of his throat and made him gag.

He forced his way through the roiling, boiling stew, his face screwed up like a baby's face just before it cries. Whatever monster was waiting for him on the other side of this, he thought, it couldn't be much worse than this.

And this just kept getting worse and worse.

As he walked through the mess, the lightning flashed again. Rick let out a strangled moan of pure, wretched nausea. In the momentary light of the flash, he could see the substance through which he was moving. It was horrible . . . horrible. Those chunks of filth that kept swimming over him—they were alive! Bug-eyed little lobstery monsters with chattering fangs and claws, they bit and snapped at him as they went past, and when his armor repulsed them, the beasts let off an angry little puff of stink and slithered away.

When the lightning flashed out, the creatures became invisible again in the darkness. Which was equally horrific! Knowing they were there, feeling them take their little nips at him, smelling their awfulness. And just as Rick was praying to get to the other side of this thing . . .

Boom. Boom. Boom.

Even in the darkness, he began to make out the even darker darkness beyond the soupy wall: the hulking shape of the giant that was waiting for him, guarding the interface.

And now, the cloud began to thin. The soupy substance was becoming mist again. Rick could feel the walk grow easier. Fewer chunks and creatures touched him. The smell began to abate. His nausea receded. He started taking full breaths again. He was almost relieved.

Then the lightning struck and the thunder rolled at once, and in a single instant, the mist was gone and he got his first clear look at the King of the Dead.

———

Favian flashed through the graveyard mist. Even he was surprised he had the nerve to do it. Graveyards spooked him out. Mist spooked him out. Darkness spooked him out. Just about everything spooked him out if he had to do it alone.

But he had to do it, so he did. He flashed through the misty cemetery, simply ignoring whatever ghouls and zombies were probably right that minute circling him and moving in for the kill. Even the sight of the cloud wall in front of him didn't make him hesitate. It didn't make him happy, mind you. But though he swallowed a little harder as the flashing miasma loomed above him, he didn't stop flashing past the graves to get to it. In fact, he didn't even stop when he reached it. He figured if he let himself think about it, he'd never go through. Instead, Favian held his breath and flashed right into the cloud . . .

Or, that is, he would have. Except when he hit the wall of cloud, it was like hitting a brick wall, and he was flung backward and fell on his backside with an impact that jarred even a light-made creature like himself.

Favian got up. He floated in front of the boiling wall. He tried again to get through it—and again, it was like hitting brick.

At that moment, finally, all his anger against Rick dissipated. He realized the truth: Now that he wanted to help his friend, he couldn't. As the cloud wall kept out the water that carried Mariel, so it also kept out light like the light he was made of. Only the more solid Rick could pass through the barrier.

Whatever happened in there, it was going to happen to Rick alone.

———

Mariel had never felt anything like what she was feeling now. As she flowed through the stream around the grave-yard, fresh energy and fresh strength seemed to pour into her. But it wasn't just that. Suddenly, she knew things, remembered things she had never known or remembered before. Rick loved her. And she loved Rick. And they were going to be together. The idea made her feel a kind of happiness she had never in her life felt before.

And yet how could it be true? When Rick said she was not even a human being. She was just a code coming out of a black box. How was it possible . . . ?

An idea came to her . . . She slowed in her passage.

Hurry, a voice said inside her. *Rick . . .*

That voice . . . Mariel realized it was her voice, her thoughts, and yet . . . yet it also wasn't.

Who are you? she thought.

The voice spoke back to her: *I am Mariel.*

And with a hundred images and sensations and memories crashing in on her all at once, Mariel thought, *I am Molly.*

Mariel did not understand completely, but she understood enough: She would not die in this place; she would not die alone; she would not lose the hero who had come to help her, the man she had come to love. She didn't know how—not really—but it was going to be all right.

If only she could reach Rick in time.

With renewed energy she flowed on in the little stream . . .

. . . until she, too, reached the wall of fog and was blocked by it and could go no farther.

As he stepped out of the fog cloud, Rick found himself in a nowhere netherworld. He was standing on a floating circular platform of rock with nothing around it but starry darkness. It was a kind of arena, he thought, maybe as big as three or four football fields, but not much bigger. There'd be nowhere to run here, not for long. It was not a place made for escape. It was a place made for battle.

The only features of the floating rock were occasional jutting crags and boulders, rough stalagmites that stuck up out of the stony earth. And at the far edge, looming up high about a hundred yards, mingling with the blackness beyond the rocky arena, there was a transparent ghostly image of a face, an ugly face that looked like a cross between a toad and a skull.

Kurodar.

That was the interface: the place where Kurodar's mind connected to the Realm, the source of the Realm, and the imagination that created it.

And the King of the Dead prowled back and forth before it, ready to slaughter anyone who tried to do it harm.

Boom. Boom. Boom.

The King of the Dead was a monster. But more than that, it seemed an assembly of monsters, half a dozen monsters, their parts cut up and rearranged into something new. Its body was immense and scaly as a dragon's. It had a dinosaur tail that writhed behind it like a snake. It had slithery, squirming arms like the tentacles of an octopus.

Several of its arms were holding weapons: a gigantic sword, a huge ax, a spear the size of a tree. Rising up behind its back were two enormous purple wings, bony and webbed like the wings of a demon.

But its face—that was the most horrific thing about it.

It was a human face. A man's face. There was something particularly horrible about that, about a human face crowning that monstrosity. Cruelty and viciousness were etched deeply into every feature of it: in the narrow planes and angles of its brow and cheeks, in the bright, furious gleam of its eyes, and in the thin lips pressed together in a tight smile of sadistic pleasure. The tortured intelligence in the man's expression made it even uglier, even worse. It knew what it was, what a beast it was, and its only possible joy could be destruction.

It spotted Rick the moment he stepped out of the cloud wall. Its tight smile widened. Its bright eyes grew brighter still.

"You!" he said—and his deep voice rolled like the thunder inside the cloud. And then he laughed, and the air shook all around him.

In that first moment Rick confronted the great creature, he was so struck with shock and terror, he could barely think at all. Still, though, an idea began to form in the back of his mind. It wasn't quite conscious. He wasn't completely aware of what he was thinking and he couldn't have put it into words. But even in that frightened moment, it flashed dimly through his brain that just as the Golden City was made of images from Kurodar's imagination, so, too, was this beast, this guardian of the interface, this final boss in the great deadly video game that was MindWar. The monster was a combination of every monster Rick had met and battled in this cursed Realm. Its wings were the wings that Reza had had in the fortress; its snake-like tail belonged to the Spider-Snake; its octopus arms were the arms of the Octo-Guardian Rick had battled in the Realm's black outer space . . .

. . . and so the face . . . the face, too, must belong to someone . . .

But before the thought could fully form, the King of the Dead attacked him. One of its slithery arms whipped back and forward and hurled the tree-sized spear right at him.

It happened so quickly, Rick barely had time even to think of getting out of the way. Then he did think it—and the moment the thought crossed his mind, he found himself moving suddenly in a Favian-like flash.

Whoa!

It was the power of Mariel's armor, he realized, magnifying his spirit and turning his thoughts to instantaneous action.

He flashed to the side in a silver streak and the spear fell where he had just been standing, its point smashing through the rock so that it stuck in the arena floor, its shaft shivering. Rick stared at the weapon that now pierced the ground where, a second ago, he had been standing. But before he could fully register the nearness of his escape, the King of the Dead flew at him.

One flap of its giant wings that stirred the mist to swirling and it was in the air, its great bulk lifting off the floor of the rock arena with preternatural grace. It let out a roar and . . .

Oh no! Rick thought.

. . . breathed out a gout of fire. The claws of its dragon feet extended like daggers as it plummeted down toward him, and another of its octopus arms snapped the edge of a gigantic ax at Rick's head.

There was nowhere for Rick to go. If he dashed to the right, the ax would cut him down; to the left, the claws would impale him. Run away and the beast's breath of flame would scorch him to cinders.

There was nothing else for him to do: he charged straight at the thing.

Again, his armor turned his very thought to action. Even as the King of Death flew at him through the air, he was flashing forward like a silver beam of light. He passed underneath the monster just before it landed. And when it did land, the thunderous tremor that shook the arena sent Rick spilling face-forward onto the rock.

The rough surface of the arena floor would have scraped his flesh off, but the armor protected him. Good thing, too, because he was able to leap up just in time to dodge the King of the Dead's lashing tail. He leapt to his feet—and then leapt into the air as the spiny tail swept under him. By the time Rick dropped to the surface again, the King of the Dead had spun round to face him.

"You think you'll escape me?" the thing said. There was something particularly horrible about watching that human face speak human words atop the body of a monster. He had a thick Russian accent, like Kurodar's own. "They all thought they'd escape me! But they all fell into my prison eventually and into my hands. Look around, boy! There is no place for you to run!"

With that, the creature let out another great roar, its face tilted toward the starry nothingness. Breathed fire blotted out even the color of the dark. It spread its slithery tentacles out on all sides like the arms of a flattened spider. And its front—disgustingly—opened. And it released smaller monsters from within its belly.

Boars and Harpies and Cobras—they rushed and slithered and flew at Rick across the rocky arena. His sword was in his hand and with the armor giving him speed and strength, he flashed from place to place, swinging the blade and cutting the creatures down. Harpies fell from the sky and died. Boars reeled back, cut in half. Cobras shattered, their white bones flying . . .

But while Rick was distracted with the melee, the enormous King of the Dead thundered at him again, the pound of its huge feet making the round platform quake.

The beast reached him . . . towered over him . . . whipped its gigantic sword at his midsection. Rick had just dispatched the final Boar in quick combat, and only the power he got from Mariel's armor gave him the speed he needed to duck the King's giant blade. He felt the great wind of it as it passed over his head. Then he straightened—and struck back. He flashed straight at the King of the Dead, bringing his sword back with both hands and swinging it around like a baseball bat. Tall as Rick was, his head only came up to the monster's knee. Mariel's blade sank into the scaly calf of the beast. It roared fire and slapped at Rick with a slithery arm.

The blow caught Rick on the side of the head and sent him flying. He landed hard on the rock surface, dazed. The transparent head of Kurodar—the interface—rose up above him. Did he have time to attack it while the King of the Dead was hobbled by his wound?

He glanced away from the interface and toward the beast. He saw the place where his blade had sunk into the King of the Dead's leg. There was a gash there, bleeding green goo, and the King was still roaring in pain. But even as Rick looked at it, the wound began to mend itself. In a second, it was completely gone. The King was healed and whole again and ready to renew his attack.

No time to attack the interface. He had to stop the King of the Dead first.

Rick pushed up to his feet, breathing hard. He could feel Mariel's armor bleeding strength into him through the pores of his skin, but it couldn't save him forever. He was growing tired already and would soon grow more tired still. And the King . . . he had so much power! Too much! He could heal himself. He could create monsters of his own. He was ten times Rick's size and a hundred times more powerful. Rick's armor was strong and his sword was sharp, but he needed some other power to defeat this thing.

You hold the truth inside you. The truth is your greatest weapon.

What truth? he wondered. But there was no time to find the answer now. With a fiery roar, the King of the Dead opened himself once again and set another army of creatures at him—and flew into the air and attacked Rick at the same time.

Rick flashed away, the Boars and Harpies and Cobras coming after him, the King of the Dead shaking the stony platform so hard, it nearly knocked Rick over. For the next several minutes, there was nothing in Rick's mind but the swing of his sword and the flash of his movements. Only when all the smaller creatures were dead and he confronted the King face-to-face again could he begin to try to think this through.

The wall of cloud was at his back, and the King of the Dead stood before him.

You must learn what Kurodar does not know, Baba Yaga had told him. *You must face the horror he cannot face.*

This place—this MindWar Realm—was so full of horror, Rick hardly knew where to begin. But while he had been fighting, it seemed, his mind had been working on the problem unconsciously. And now, as the King of the

Dead ground its teeth and roared more fire and spread its wings ready to fly at him again, images and ideas flashed through Rick's brain faster than he could understand them.

The Realm was made from Kurodar's imagination. He created most of it purposefully. But here in the Golden City, some things seemed to have come to life spontaneously whether Kurodar wanted them to or not.

Even I'm his creature, poor soul that I am, Baba Yaga had said. *But he can't touch me. He can't make me leave, much as he may want to.*

So some parts of Kurodar's imagination were beyond his own control. He had made this great beast, the King of the Dead, on purpose . . .

In the image of his father!

The thought came into Rick's mind suddenly and he knew it was true. He remembered that vision Baba Yaga had given him. All the dead of the Soviet Union, the murdered dissenters who did not want the fake paradise that was being forced upon them.

They all thought they'd escape me! But they all fell into my prison eventually and into my hands.

That was the King of the Dead speaking, but he was speaking in the voice of Kurodar's brutal father, the agent of the KGB. A man who had murdered so many. A man so hated by the people that when the Soviet Union fell, a mob had beaten him to death, right in front of his son . . .

In the same flash in which he remembered this, Rick remembered his own anger against his father when he

thought his dad had betrayed his family, before he understood that his father had made, instead, the impossible
choice of sacrifice, the impossible sacrifice of love.

But what if that had not been his dad? What if his dad
had been a monster like this? What if his dad had had no
God to teach him that sacrificial love but had known only
the god of his own power? How hard it would have been
then for Rick to find his trust again. . . . to rebuild his lost
boy-faith into the faith of a man. His dad's love . . . his
mom's love. . . Raider's love . . . Molly's . . . It had all been
God's love and had brought God's love to him—that was
the love that now surrounded him like Mariel's armor and
made him strong.

But what if there had been no love? What if he had
been Kurodar?

The King of the Dead roared and the Realm's black sky
was lit by fire. It spread its demon wings and whiplashed
its octopus arms. It lashed its snake tail and pounded its
dragon feet. And it charged at Rick where Rick stood
pinned against the wall of cloud.

. . . *the horror he can't face* . . .

"He was glad!" Rick shouted. "He was glad when they
killed you! You filled his heart with hate and he hated you
and he was glad!"

It was so strange. The words came out of him and they
were only words, but he felt them fly from him like bullets. Because they were true. That was the horror Kurodar
couldn't face. He had turned his father into an evil god to

keep from facing his hatred for him, to keep himself from knowing what he truly felt when he saw his father die.

Kurodar was glad. Kurodar had been taught nothing but humiliation and beating and hatred and he was full of hatred himself, and so he was glad when his father was mobbed and humiliated and beaten to death.

"He was glad when you died!" Rick shouted.

The King of the Dead stopped his charge midway. The great monster stood in the center of the rock arena and swayed on his feet and reeled in confusion.

Rick seized the moment and launched himself at the thing. He swung Mariel's sword, and again the blade bit into the monster's scales and the creature bled green goo.

This time, Rick was ready for the King's counterattack. He ducked the sweeping tentacle and pulled the blade free and spun away.

But if he thought the battle was over, if he thought mere words would bring the giant down, he was wrong. As quickly as before, the King of the Dead healed. As quickly as before, he turned. He roared and there was fire, just as before. Nothing had changed.

Or wait . . .

Rick stood now with the interface behind him and the King of the Dead between him and the wall of fog. The monster was facing him, just as huge and powerful as before. But something was different.

The wall. The fog. It was coming undone.

The towering storm-tossed wall of fog was unfolding

from its heights and rolling down and growing smaller and thinning to mere mist as it fell. Something in Rick's words had broken through the miasma and begun to clear it away.

Rick did not have time to wonder what this could mean, or how it might help him, because the King of the Dead had spread its wings and tentacles again, and the smaller monsters were already crawling out of its belly ready to attack.

Rick braced himself for the onslaught, his sword in his two hands. And as he did, the wall of cloud unraveled completely and dissolved to drifting tendrils of white smoke and was gone. The air was clear.

It was like a dam bursting. The moment the cloud wall fell, a powerful rush of silver water and blue light came pouring into the dark that surrounded the arena. The next moment, even before the fresh spate of Boars and Harpies and Cobras could launch at him over the rocky surface, Mariel and Favian were there. Mariel rose up out of the silver flow that rushed into the rocks, and Favian burst like an angel from the powerful blue beam that pierced the darkness.

The water spirit was on the King of the Dead's left and the blue sprite was to the right of him. The King of the Dead turned one way and the other in surprise and rage.

The army of Boars and Harpies and Cobras rushed and flew and slithered over the arena toward Rick—but even as they charged, Mariel threw out both her arms at once and unleashed a powerful flood of shining mercurial water. It washed over the entire stampeding army and in the next second they were carried away. They were gone.

The King of the Dead let out one last shrieking cry and spread its wings and rose up off the platform into the air.

But now Favian threw out his hands and blue light shot from his palms to form a barrier. The King flew at it, struck it, and, giant though he was, fell back. The arena shook as the monster dropped down onto it. And now Mariel turned her power on him, and surrounded him with silver water, hemming him into the small circle at its center.

"The interface, Rick!" she cried out.

And at the sound of that almost musical voice, Rick roused himself from his startled shock. He saw Mariel's substance circling the beast. He saw Favian's light barring its way.

He turned around. There, framed against the backdrop of starry emptiness, Kurodar's twisted, pain-racked face hovered above him.

The thing was too big and insubstantial to attack with his sword alone. But now he remembered: that final power, the last upgrade, the blast he had unleashed in the church against the swarming armies of the dead . . .

He summoned the energy for that blast. He felt the charge mount within him, magnified somehow by Mariel's armor. Soon he was full of the seething strength of his faith and spirit.

And in a single blinding explosion of light and power, he released it in a great flash at the interface . . .

———

"There they are!" shouted Chuck.

The Traveler and Professor Jameson and Miss Ferris looked at the screen to see the white figure that was Rick Dial become visible again. The blue figure of Favian was there, too, and the silver figure of Mariel.

Professor Jameson turned to look at where Molly lay on the cot, her hands folded on her chest, her eyes gazing emptily up at the ceiling.

"She's broken through," he murmured.

"And look!" said Miss Ferris.

They all turned to her and then followed her gaze and they all saw the big screen with the Battle Station on it, the sky weapon that Kurodar had seized.

"The energy bar. It's not filling anymore," Miss Ferris said.

"They've done it," the Traveler murmured. He glanced at Professor Jameson, nodded toward Molly. "Take her off the box. She's done enough. Bring her back."

Professor Jameson nodded once and hurried to his daughter. Gently, he lifted the band off her forehead and unplugged it from the black box.

Molly went on staring another second. Then blinked once. Then looked at him. Then smiled radiantly.

The Traveler turned calmly back to his computer to finish programming the portal.

———

In the moments before Kurodar died, he didn't feel surprised. It was really as if he'd always known who he was, what he was, and what he was trying to hide from himself. It was as if when Rick shouted out the truth inside his mind, he merely nodded and surrendered, all the will to power going out of him, because he knew all the power in the world wouldn't save him from the awful fate of being himself.

Strapped to his chair and wired to his machine, the electricity that backed up into him when the interface was destroyed was really no more painful than the hatred that had seethed inside him all along, as if his veins were filled with acid or boiling water.

The native workers who had tended and fed him out of fear this whole long time ran for their lives screaming as the machinery that generated the Realm began to rock and smoke in the moments before it exploded.

But Kurodar didn't move. He couldn't, attached to the mechanism as he was, part of the mechanism as he was. He just sat there and waited for the final blast.

And in the end, he died weeping.

———

After he struck the deathblow, Rick watched the face of Kurodar come raining down out of the black sky in points of twinkling light. It was almost beautiful, though he knew it heralded destruction. He turned around and his eyes locked with the eyes of the King of the Dead. For another moment, the great beast struggled and writhed, trapped within Mariel's silver circle of water and barred by Favian's rays of blue light. For another moment, its eyes, the eyes of Kurodar in the face of his father, burned with hatred and with rage.

But the next moment, Rick saw the fire of that hatred go out, and he knew that Kurodar was finished.

The King of the Dead threw back its human head and roared in agony. Its dragon body twisted and its demon wings crumbled to red ash. It shuddered once and then its whole body erupted into flame. Rick could see the smaller monsters—the Boars and Harpies and Cobras—burning to ashes inside it.

In seconds, the fire consumed the monster and the King of the Dead rained down out of the air in a black storm of ashes. Even before those ashes settled to the rock circle of the arena, the night around them began to quake.

Rick knew what would happen before it happened and then he saw it begin. The graveyard in the distance and the Golden City beyond it began to accordion together, collapsing in on themselves and all of it rushing toward him, toward the blackness that was going to consume it all.

The MindWar Realm was dying, all of it, falling into the emptiness that surrounded it, becoming nothing as Kurodar died.

Rick looked at Mariel, who hung silver in the air above him. He looked at Favian, who floated just above the arena. The three of them exchanged glances as the Realm collapsed around them, knowing the falling world would take them with it into the darkness, that they had only a minute left to live, if that.

Then, as they gazed their good-byes at one another, the portal opened in the middle of them: a floating diamond of purple light.

Rick was surprised by the depth of his sadness at the sight of it. He knew he had to go through—his life lay that way. But the thought of leaving Mariel behind here, losing her forever, made him hesitate even so.

Mariel inclined her head toward him. "Go on," she said.

Favian cried out in a simple anguish of sorrow: "Mariel! You said you'd come."

She shook her head. She gave a small, sad smile. "I said that Rick and I will be together and we will be. Don't be afraid. Nothing that truly lives in me will ever die. Go home and you'll find me there."

The Golden City crumbled and the ruins of it rushed toward them where they stood surrounded by blackness. A great wind of destruction began to wash over them.

Rick stepped toward the portal.

"Favian," he said.

Favian shook his head no, but all the same, he began moving too.

They both stepped to the portal. They both kept their eyes on Mariel hovering above them. The MindWar Realm came collapsing in on them. The blackness folded over them.

The last sight Rick had of Mariel was her smiling at him: a sad smile of good-bye.

Then he stepped through the portal as the world came tumbling down around him.

EPILOGUE: GAME OVER

WHEN RICK OPENED his eyes, he was alone in his bedroom. He blinked up at the ceiling, confused.

Was it just another dream? he wondered. *Was it all a dream from the beginning?*

He swung his legs off the bed to the floor, and the ache that went through them reminded him: No, some of it was real, at least. Some of it was all too real.

He moved to the window. He pulled back the curtains. He looked out.

A heavy snow was falling on the MindWar compound. The ground and the rooftops were already carpeted with white and so was the forest beyond the fence. It almost managed to make the place look pleasant.

Almost Christmas, Rick thought.

Through the swirling flakes, Rick could see the guards clustered around the gate. He could see the fence was damaged from where Molly's truck had hit it when she tried to escape. He could see the tower where the Boar had broken through the Breach and killed the guard. The thought made him touch the side of his forehead. He checked his mind. The portal inside him was gone. Kurodar was gone.

It wasn't a dream. It all happened, he thought. *It was all real.*

His mind flashed back to the end of it: the stone arena in the midst of space, the gigantic King of the Dead, the cloud wall collapsing at the sound of his voice, Favian, Mariel . . .

The sadness he had felt at the end came back to him. Mariel. She had died with the MindWar Realm. And Victor One. Lost in the battle outside the gate.

Rick stood at the window watching the snow. He felt very much alone.

There was a rapid knock at the door. Running his fingers up through his hair, Rick moved toward it. But before he reached it, the door sprang open and there was his little brother, Raider, too full of energy to wait for him.

"Aren't you coming? You've been asleep for hours! You gonna sleep forever? Everyone's here! Everyone's waiting for you!"

The eager pie-plate face beamed up at him and Rick smiled, heavyhearted. Whatever the kid was drinking, he needed a glass. Probably everyone needed a glass.

"Come on, Rick!" the kid said, grabbing him by the hand and pulling.

"All right, all right," said Rick. "Take it easy. My legs."

But Raider did not take it easy. He kept pulling and Rick stumbled after him, out the door, down the hall.

They were waiting in the living room, all of them, arrayed in various places beneath the Christmas tree. The tree's colored lights played over them and so did the lights strung along the mantelpiece. The small manger scene on the coffee table seemed almost alive in the moving light from the flames in the fireplace.

His mom and dad were standing by the fire together. Molly was in the wing chair by the tree.

"There he is: the man of the hour, awake at last," Rick's father said.

His mother applauded comically. Molly laughed.

Miss Ferris was sitting on the sofa with her back to Rick. She turned to look at him over her shoulder when Raider pulled him in, and she almost smiled.

A man was sitting beside her. He stood up to greet Rick—a small but sturdy-looking black guy with worried eyes: Fabian Child. Favian. He came up around the sofa, his hand extended. Rick grabbed his hand and shook it and then pulled him into a rough hug.

When Fabian drew back, there were tears in his eyes. He shook Rick's hand again. "You did it, man. You did it!"

"Well," said Rick, "we all did it. I could never have beaten that thing alone."

"Yeah, but you're the one who brought us back. I should have known you would never leave her behind. I'm sorry I doubted you."

Rick opened his mouth to answer, but he wasn't sure what to say. Fabian saw his uncertainty and gestured across the room at Molly.

"She made it, man. She made it through."

Molly stood up and moved across the room to Rick. Rick didn't understand what Fabian was saying, and then Molly came closer and he looked into her eyes and he sort of did understand, though he couldn't have explained it.

Nothing that truly lives in me will ever die.

That's what Mariel had said in the end. And Rick knew that that's what Victor One would have said, too, if he were here. And he was here. And so was Mariel. Rick didn't understand it, but he knew it was so.

And he knew that Molly was with him, and he wrapped his arms around her and held her close, and the sadness in his heart was somehow gone. He looked past her at where his father and mother stood next to the tree, smiling at them both. He remembered how, before all this started, he had thought he had lost everything. He had thought his life was over. How wrong he had been. How little he had understood.

Nothing that truly lives in me will ever die.

Molly drew back a little in his arms and looked up at him. He said her name and kissed her.

The MindWar was over. They had won.

READING GROUP GUIDE

1. Were you surprised by the reveal of the traitor? Do you think their reasons were justified? Would you have made the same choice? Why or why not?

2. Ivan Doshenko grew up filled with hate and bitterness. His anger built into obsessional rage, which turned him into Kurodar. His father never taught him love, just humiliation. Have you ever allowed hate to take over your life? How did you eliminate it?

3. Throughout the novel, Kurodar is set on vengeance against America. Why do you believe so many people dislike America? What was Kurodar's reason? Do you find it to be valid?

4. Kurodar's father believed that killing others could create equality and paradise. Who else in history has believed this?

5. Sadly, Kurodar felt he deserved his father's abuse. Many victims of abuse feel this way. How is this line of thinking flawed? Do you think Kurodar was justified in his beliefs?

6. Rick has a poignant moment where he realizes his dad never abandoned him, as he once thought. How does his dad's sacrificial love compare to God's love for us? What are some differences and similarities?

7. Rick's mother tells him, "You'll never go anywhere alone. I promise." What did she mean by that statement? How does that knowledge help Rick in the Realm? Can this reminder help you in *your* daily life?

8. Commander Mars was an intelligent and powerful man, yet he was not immune to corruption. How did his pride ultimately lead to his downfall?

9. Favian is a worrier by nature, but he could be a warrior when needed. How is it possible to be both? What can we do to overcome our worries?

10. Rick comes to realize the impact that God had on his dad and how, without his love, the Traveler could have become like Kurodar's dad. How can God's love change a person, such as it did in this story?

11. Rick tells Molly, "Let not your heart be troubled," as the Bible states. It brought him comfort as he prepared for the battle of his life in the Realm. How can this verse be a comfort to you?

12. Molly states in the story, "In a video game, you can die one hundred times, but you only have to get it right once. In the Realm you can get it right one hundred times, but if you die once, it's game over." Chuck agrees, saying it's just like real life. What

are some ways Rick and Molly make the most of their one life? What can you do to make the most of yours?

13. Mariel gives Rick armor in the Realm to increase his power. She tells him, "It won't make you invulnerable. Everyone is vulnerable to injury and death. But as long as your faith stays strong, it will give you more power than you ever knew you had." What are some examples from the story of Rick's faith staying strong? What are some examples from your own life?

14. Did you find this story to be a satisfying conclusion to the trilogy? If not, what would you have done differently?

CHARLIE WEST JUST WOKE UP IN SOMEONE ELSE'S NIGHTMARE.

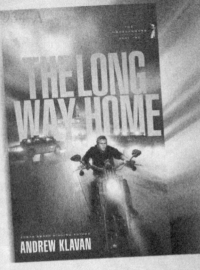

THE HOMELANDERS SERIES

AVAILABLE IN PRINT AND E-BOOK